TANYA ANDERS

Mated to the Orc Guard

Orc Bride Fated Mates 3

Contents

Foreword   iv

Chapter One   1

Chapter Two   17

Chapter Three   26

Chapter Four   36

Chapter Five   51

Chapter Six   63

Chapter Seven   80

Chapter Eight   108

Chapter Nine   125

Chapter Ten   142

Chapter Eleven   159

Chapter Twelve   173

Chapter Thirteen   190

Chapter Fourteen   229

Epilogue   243

Foreword

Mated to the Orc Guard contains steamy scenes. It is intended for an adult audience.

Orc Bride Fated Mates Series

Book 1 - Taken by the Orc Warrior
Book 2 - Given to the Orc Hunter
Book 3 - Mated to the Orc Guard

Chapter One

I was lying in a fetal position, balled up in the corner of my basement cell in the convent.

I didn't even have a blanket to cover myself. I was often debilitated by cold, and the way I preferred to protect my body (from bugs and the chill) was to wrap myself into a snug little ball of despair.

I was imprisoned in my own personal hell, in both my mind and physical surroundings.

I tried not to wallow too often in the cloak of my gloom.

Some days were better than others. On good days, I could keep to my prayer schedule and harbor the hope of release to rejoin my sworn sisters in the daily life of the convent. But on other days, I could barely bring myself to lift my head off the ground, much less do anything else.

I knew it wasn't healthy for me to lie around. Sometimes, I would roam the tiny cell — if nothing else but for the exercise. I found that I felt better when I did that, and wasn't as dreadfully stiff and fatigued once the next day rolled around.

It was especially chilly tonight. The basement floor was icy cold, and the scant light that filtered in beneath the door from the hallway did little to lighten the perpetual gloom. On the days when I despaired the most, I felt like I was slowly dying.

But I refused to give up completely. There *had* to be a way out of this nightmare. I would not allow my last embers of hope to be extinguished.

I sought refuge in prayer. I kept in touch with the Almighty, remembering my teaching that, although we are tested, God does not give us more than we can handle.

Even through my misery, my faith never faltered — not once. God was good — all the time. Any suffering I endured would only help me come out stronger and better prepared for the storms ahead.

The very first lesson I was taught when I entered the convent as a girl, by the wonderfully wise and benevolent Sister Geneville, was about the ebb and flow of the tide of life. Sometimes it would lift me up, sometimes it would carry me out to sea, where the unforgiving waves would thrash me mercilessly. Either way, my task was always to keep my head above water.

I was on the edge of despair, with little strength left, but I wouldn't drown — because Sister Geneville's patience and wisdom had made me a strong swimmer, metaphorically. I couldn't afford to view myself as a victim, regardless of how bleak the situation seemed. This was simply the violent swell before calm waters beckoned on the tide of life.

But I had to admit, in my current state, the waves appeared more foreboding than ever — how could they not? I was surrounded by a musky, damp, frigid darkness that clung to my body and spirit like a sinister claw — a claw that kept tightening its grip on me day by day.

No matter how fervently I tried to chase away my inner demons, which wanted me to succumb to despair, they always found a way back into my consciousness; tormenting me, torturing me, taunting me.

I looked to God in my darkest hour, and remembered the lined yet radiant face of Sister Geneville. She would gently cup my face in her warm, wrinkled hands and kiss my forehead on the many occasions I sought her solace, when I felt I could no longer cope with the austere life of a convent sister.

Tonight, I was in a restless state. My teeth were chattering and goose bumps raised their little prickles on the surface of my skin.

I was fitful. I couldn't make heads nor tails of what time it was. The days and nights had begun to blend together recently, forming a convoluted mess of time that disconnected me from reality.

I gave up on sleep, remembering the latest note I had been writing using the quill, parchment and small pot of ink that luckily remained in the cell from when it was used as a study chamber.

I glanced over at the door with caution, licked my lips nervously and pulled the slip of parchment, ink and quill out of the hole where I had hidden it in the wall.

Writing was my escape, my way to vent without a listening ear to hear my troubles. It was part of the reason why I had maintained my sanity, and I figured now was as good a time as any to get some of that pent-up turmoil out of my head.

Approaching the door, I dropped to my knees and placed the parchment on the ground to use the hazy light that seeped in underneath. I found where I had left off, then began writing:

Mercifully, a quill and parchment remain in this cell from when it was used as a study chamber.

I am thus able to write what I fear may be my final message.

I wrote a few more lines then looked up in alarm as I heard footsteps echoing in the corridor outside. They reverberated like thunder in the confined space — these were not human footsteps; that much was abundantly clear. My heart began racing as panic gripped me. I hastily scribbled down a few more lines.

I must write in haste now as I hear footsteps thundering in the corridor outside . . . They do not sound human...

I kept writing furiously as the dreadful noise became louder. The thunderous footsteps bellowed down the hall, sending a foreboding rumble through the walls. The sound reverberated through my eardrums and pounded like a gong in my heart. I held my breath and broke out in a cold, nervous sweat that made me feel both icy and hot all over. I channeled my despair into my writing hand.

I know not what horrors await me on the other side of the door, but I shall put my faith in the Almighty for salvation...

The crashing footsteps were suddenly silent — the creature had reached my door. I could hear female voices now, just outside. My heart in my throat, I quickly finished up my note.

Please know this about me...I lived...I loved the Lord and my sisters.

Chapter One

My heart was pure...and my name was Sister Hana...

I folded the note and quickly slipped it back into the cavity in the wall, along with the quill and ink pot. Then I backed away into a far corner of the cell.

A terrible screeching sound rang out as the rusty door bolts were released and slowly slid out of their catches.

My heart galloped. My stomach twisted into knots, churning with trepidation. Clammy sweat created a film on my skin.

The door sprung open in one sweeping movement. Light flooded into the room.

In walked Vitora, the resident Mother Superior. Vitora had been anointed just over a year ago when the previous Mother Superior had met a gruesome death.

Every muscle in my body froze with fear as soon as I laid eyes on her. Vitora was vicious. She was capable of unspeakable acts of cruelty to anyone unlucky enough to face her wrath. She knew no mercy. Her hate and spite were legendary.

Upon her ascension, she was given a solemn duty by the Archdiocese to protect the sisters in her convent. Instead, she seemed to derive a thrill from making them feel devoid of faith, malnourished and mistreated. If you crossed an invisible line with her, you could kiss any hope of freedom (or a warm belly full of food) goodbye.

She looked like a vile, wretched witch. Her coal black eyes were devoid of life — like she was dead inside. She was the kind of woman who robbed even the air around her of happiness. She shrouded everything and everyone she crossed paths with in a veil of darkness. That darkness began crawling over me like an army of insects every time she came near me.

When she entered my cell, our eyes locked, but I quickly

averted mine, lest I be drawn into the void.

Vitora wasn't alone. She was flanked by two high-ranking Senior Sisters. My eyes trailed over them briefly, before I became distracted by the huge, menacing beast that entered the room behind them. It was an ogre.

The ogre was the most disgusting, atrocious thing I'd ever seen. It towered over all of us. It wasn't human in height, but as tall as a small building. Its dirt-stained hands were so massive that I had no doubt they could snap me (or any of us in the cell, for that matter) in half like a twig.

The ogre had a brutish snarl on its ugly face. Stomach-souring drool dribbled down the side of its wrinkly chin. It was so huge in stature that it had to slump its posture and bow its head just to fit inside the room. The ogre's black eyes were even emptier than Vitora's — if that were possible.

Its elvish ears stuck out with pointy tips. The top of its head was mainly bald, aside from a few strings and tufts of toffee-colored hair.

It wore only a black loin covering around its waist, resembling a kilt. Its knees were wrinkly and caked with dirt, as were its giant, shoeless feet. It had long arms that awkwardly dangled by its sides. Its flesh wasn't muscular, but drooping and weathered, and covered in grime.

It made a detestable grunting noise as its eyes scanned the room and landed on me with a famished expression. I saw an eagerness flickering in its eyes that paralyzed me with dread.

I stared between each of them. I couldn't speak even if I wanted to. My constricted throat wouldn't allow any words to escape. It was the most intense sense of fear that I'd ever experienced.

Myrah, one of the Senior Sisters, had an amused expression

on her pock-marked face. Her skin was pale and her cheek-bones high. Red hair cascaded down her back and framed her gaunt face. Her brown eyes twinkled with mischief. I could sense an eagerness to inflict suffering — a common trait among Senior Sisters.

Myrah was feared and despised by many of the lower-ranking sisters, myself included. I did my best to stay under her radar. She was a longstanding Senior Sister who had always mindlessly supported the corruption of the higher-ups. She was proudly standing to Vitora's right.

To her left was Elisse. She was a new Senior Sister, having been elevated to the ranks shortly after Vitora became Mother Superior. I didn't know much about her, but she was no doubt as malevolent as the others. In fact, it seemed that cruelty and callousness were prerequisites to join their little cabal. No doubt Vitora looked for these 'qualities' when selecting her underlings.

Vitora took a step closer to me, wielding her treasured nine-tailed dragon whip, which she had inherited from her predecessor. It was designed to inflict the maximum amount of pain and suffering to those unfortunate enough to find themselves at the sharp end of it.

As she narrowed the gap between us, I instinctively drew back, cowering away from her. I didn't want her anywhere near me. She made my skin crawl just by looking at me with the malevolent darkness set deep in her irises.

"Here she is," Vitora said, in a bright voice, pointing to me as she addressed the ogre over her shoulder.

The ogre's coal eyes flickered hungrily.

I wasn't going to surrender to this massive beast, if that was what Vitora had in mind. I would fight until I died, if I had to.

I'd rather be dead than at the whim of this animal.

I offered a silent prayer for the light of the Holy Spirit to surround and protect me.

The ogre made another detestable grunting noise before it spoke.

"Is she pure and clean, as I asked?" His deep voice rumbled like thunder in the enclosed quarters, making all the women, myself included, jump.

I found his words bleakly ironic. He was inquiring about my cleanliness, when ogres were the mostly filthy creatures in existence — both physically and mentally. This particular ogre was doing very little to change that widely-held opinion.

As the newly-appointed Senior Sister, Elisse wasted no time in jumping at the chance to impress Vitora.

"I'll check her over," Elisse chimed, skirting across the small cell to reach me in no time.

Elisse was tall with bright green eyes and chestnut hair. She had a darkly eager look in her eyes — a kind of hunger that conveniently blinded you to your morals (if you had any) so you could get ahead in life.

As a nun, I wasn't supposed to harbor hate for anyone in my heart, especially my own sworn sisters. But I would be lying if I said I didn't loath Vitora and her atrocious minions.

I opened my mouth to command Elisse not to lay a single finger on me but, before I could get a word in edgewise, she reached her slender hands out and quickly pulled my tunic up over my head.

She snatched the garment off my body so forcefully that I was afraid it might be ripped and unsalvageable when I tried to put it back on…*if* I even got that chance.

"Turn around," Elisse demanded, throwing my tunic to the

dirty floor and roughly handling me without a moment of hesitation or empathy.

I flinched and instinctively draped my arms around my naked breasts in a feeble attempt to cover my body. I crossed my legs together and tightly squeezed, attempting to conceal my private parts, but it was too late.

My full body had already been revealed in plain sight and here I stood, naked and humiliated in front of three women and an ogre. I felt intense shame heat up my face when all four of them began staring at my flesh with fascination.

Elisse said something, but I was too dazed with shock and humiliation to register it.

"Wh-what?" I gawked at Elisse, casting her a blank stare.

She gave me a stony expression. "You heard me. *Turn. Around.*" She made an abrupt swiveling motion with her index finger.

I slowly turned around, grateful to at least hide the front of my naked body for a moment.

"Her body looks clean enough," Elisse informed Vitora after a few moments.

I caste Elisse a pitiful glance over my shoulder.

She plugged her nose by pinching the bridge of it with her thumb and index finger.

"Although she smells like she could use a good scrubbing," she added.

Vitora stepped forward to take a closer look.

"Turn back around," Elisse instructed, forcefully.

I flinched and stiffened, hesitating. The hesitation cost me.

Myrah sprang forward past Elisse and grabbed a fist-full of my hair. She yanked it so hard that I stumbled, desperately trying to regain my balance so I wouldn't crumple to the floor.

It seemed Myrah had enough of Elisse monopolizing the proceedings. She wanted a chance in the limelight too, and was keen to show Vitora that she could be equally as effective as Elisse in taking the initiative.

My scalp seared in pain. I winced but refused to cry out from the agony I felt. The more distress I displayed, the more satisfaction they would derive from my anguish. I didn't want to give them that victory.

"She said, *turn around*," Myrah declared, through clenched teeth, giving me a stern expression. Her anger appeared white hot, but that was probably in part because Vitora was breathing down her neck and she wanted to prove herself an able servant.

I slowly turned around, swallowing down what was left of my pride.

Myrah stepped back, with a self-satisfied smirk plastered on her pale face.

Elisse resumed her inspection of me, taking her time to scrutinize every inch of my body, poking and prodding where she deemed necessary.

She finally glanced over her shoulder at the ogre. "All looks good here."

"Good work, Elisse," Vitora said, with a rare hint of warmth in her voice.

I saw Myrah visibly stiffen at the compliment.

I couldn't believe Elisse was being commended for violating and humiliating a fellow sister. Raw, burning anger helped me to finally find my voice.

"You are shaming *yourself* more than me with your unholy actions, *sister*," I growled, giving Elisse a menacing glare that I knew wouldn't do me any good, but made me feel better about myself. "Have you no shame? Do the vows mean nothing to you?"

"Watch your tongue," Vitora interjected icily, staring sharply at me. "You aren't to speak unless directly spoken to, and only after you have been granted permission to do so."

Elisse ignored my scowl of contempt and slowly walked in a circle around me, scrutinizing me once more and no doubt hoping for extra points from Vitora.

I opened my mouth to argue but Vitora stepped forwards, tutting with disapproval, all the while tapping her whip menacingly.

"Come now Hana, you're smarter than that, girl," she said, icily.

Hot tears blinded me. I hated to show weakness in front of them. I had my pride. But Vitora was actually correct, I had to be smart, even though I'd never felt so belittled and violated in all my life.

Meanwhile, and worse still, the giant ogre was getting aroused as his dark eyes roamed the length of my naked body. I could see a huge bulge growing underneath his black loin covering.

The material was thick, but it wasn't nearly enough to hide the grotesque erection protruding out — and growing by the second. Judging from the frightening bulge, his cock was easily larger than my entire arm.

His mammoth member engorged further as Elisse poked and prodded at me, inspecting me from head to toe as if I were a prize bull to be bought at auction.

The ogre focused on my breasts, then trailed down to my exposed pussy. He was breathing heavily now, his mouth covered in drool. It looked disgusting as it pooled in the corners of his mouth and slobbered down his chin, dribbling down his bare chest where it fell and then smacked on the cold, concrete floor in a giant puddle that made me want to vomit. I was struggling to control my gag reflex. I had to look away.

Elisse aggressively brushed her fingers through my hair — then her features collapsed. Her mouth opened into an oval of shock. She began to shriek and shake her hand, squirming in front of me.

"What the Devil is the matter with you, Elisse?" asked Vitora, who took a cautious step forward, eyeing me with suspicion.

"When I pulled my hand out of her hair, it came away with tiny black bugs crawling all over it," Elisse shrieked with revulsion.

Vitora gave me a contemptuous scowl and wrinkled her nose.

Myrah, keen to get back in on the action and embellish her Senior Sister credentials, approached me and drew her hand back. Unfortunately, my reflexes weren't as quick as hers. Her palm landed on my cheek with full force. The sting of her ruthless smack rippled through my jaw and knocked the breath from my lungs.

I instinctively drew my right hand up to nurse the wounded area, but Elisse took it away and held it at my side.

"You are a filthy *animal,*" Myrah condemned. "Look at the state of you."

I swiftly freed my hand from Elisse's grip and slapped Myrah back, relishing the ferocity with which I made contact with her cheek.

"What do you *expect* me to look like when you lock me in a dungeon?" I snapped tersely.

Myrah's green eyes were loaded with shock. Her lips were pursed in a pencil-thin line. She was seething with anger. If smoke could have released from her ears, it would have. She balled her hand into a fist.

"Enough," Vitora declared, with finality.

The ogre was slapping his knee with amusement, laughing like a creature possessed. The sound rumbled through the basement. His spittle and slobber were flung throughout the room. Some of it hit Myrah in the back of the head. She screamed. I bit my tongue so I wouldn't laugh out loud.

"I like this dirty bitch's fighting spirit," the ogre proclaimed, pointing a scabbed, meaty finger at me. "She'll provide great entertainment for my tribe. She's perfect for the sport."

A chill ran up and down my spine, which had nothing to do with the frosty temperature in the cell.

"What sport?" I asked, uneasily.

I was finished with being polite. I wasn't going to adhere to Vitora's rule to only 'speak only when given permission'. My life was on the line.

"Not that it is any of *your* business, but you will be given to the ogre's tribe as payment, you insolent *cunt*," Vitora said, angry spittle flying from her lips, although not as much as the ogre had flung.

The ogre wailed with unhinged laughter now. It made me tremble from the inside out.

"The *cunt* you are referring to will be taken by my entire clan — and myself, I might add — repeatedly until we snap her in half, or she perishes," bellowed the beast. "Should she perish first, we'll probably keep going until we do snap her in two."

This revelation was especially amusing to the ogre, and he chortled with near insanity, before continuing.

"This is just a little game for *us* to enjoy, not you, filthy bitch," he roared, looking directly at me. "The sport is to wager how long you will be able to stay alive, before our fuck chain claims your final breath."

My stomach dropped. Waves of nausea slammed into my gut. My heart pounded in my throat. I became dizzy with fear.

I turned to Vitora, my mouth hanging open in shock. "How can you do this to me? You are Mother Superior. It's your job to *protect* the nuns who have sacrificed everything to be a part of this community."

Vitora approached me, giving me an icy glare. I saw pure evil lurking behind her dark eyes.

"I *am* doing this to protect the sisters, if you must know, *cunt,*" she declared.

"How can that possibly be true?" I countered, seething.

"I have recently received word that chief Morgut has been overthrown in the orc village," Vitora said.

"What does that have to do with *me* being sold to this… *monster?*"

I cut him a despising scowl.

Vitora raised her whip and, with a deft flick of her wrist, slammed it into my stomach.

"*DO NOT* insult our honored guest — I told you already, watch your mouth," she admonished.

I doubled over in pain, clutching my stomach as agony exploded across my flesh. Once again, the wind was knocked out of me and I was left gasping for air.

I looked up at Vitora, still holding my searing belly.

Her lips twisted into a satisfied smile that made my blood boil. I wished I could charge at her, bowl her over and punch her face repeatedly until it resembled a smashed melon. She deserved to pay for the inhumane way that she treated me and other sisters.

"As I said, *bitch,* I *am* protecting my convent. How *dare* you accuse me of doing otherwise," Vitora said, indignantly.

I stood up straight, glaring daggers at her. I was still panting hard from her attack, but was managing to recover as best as I could.

Vitora's smug smile made a return appearance. "With Morgut gone, the protection pact with the convent is no longer in place. A few orcs still loyal to Morgut have informed me that Nya and Sherrine...I'm sure you remember those repulsive troublemakers...are alive and well. This was hugely disappointing news for me. I was sure they would be long dead and rotting by now."

Nya. Alive! And Sherrine, too. My dear sisters are alive! Could this be true, or was this just a ploy to ensure compliance from me?

Vitora continued. "My sources tell me the vile harlots are in league with the orcs, who plan to raid the convent and free the sisters. Of course, as Mother Superior, I cannot allow this. The welfare of the sisters is my utmost priority."

She actually said this with a straight face.

"What have you done?" I hissed.

Vitora laughed in a mocking tone. "I've made a bargain with the ogres, of course! For their protection. In return, they require one nun a month to be sacrificed for their...little sport."

Vitora placed a hand on her heart, a look of solemn virtue plastered on her face. "This is an acceptable price to pay for the safety of our beloved sisters. You, Hana, have the honor of being the first."

"You can't do this to me," I pleaded. Hot tears pooled in my eyes.

"It's already done," she retorted, coolly. "You should be grateful that you can be of service to your sworn sisters. Finally, your worthless life has attained some measure of value."

This time, I didn't try to stop the tears from coming. I was shocked at the level of brutality Vitora was willing to countenance. I shook my head uncontrollably. It was unfathomable that a Mother Superior could stoop this low. Then again, this was Vitora we were talking about. A woman without a shred of virtue.

"I'm getting bored," the ogre said, irritably. "Clean up the cunt and get her ready to go tomorrow. She better not have any bugs in her hair then. And clean out that snatch, too. I want it shiny and new…ready for action." He pointed to my crotch, drool once again spilling over his thick lips.

Vitora bowed in sickening deference to the ogre. "You have my word on this, honored protector. All will be taken care of. Both the 'Cunts' will be in pristine condition for you and your noble tribe."

The ogre snorted irritably and left the room, followed by Vitora, Myrah and Elisse.

The door slammed shut and the bolts screeched into place.

I sunk to my knees and cradled my head in my hands, weeping until my shoulders shook and my eyes burned.

I was left alone in the cold, dark room — with only my destructive thoughts to keep me company.

Chapter Two

Later that evening, I was tucked, as usual, into the corner of my cell.

My eyes were absentmindedly scanning the adjacent wall. My knees were tucked up to my chest. I wasn't thinking of anything in particular, but rooted in my present sensations.

My mind had these periods of rest when it was more or less running on autopilot and I was able, briefly, to quell the deluge of bleak deliberations. Then there were the more fretful times when I couldn't shut off the cascade of destructive thoughts, no matter how fervently I tried. They enveloped me and tore at my very soul.

Naturally, I preferred the more tranquil times. It was torture being locked in the prison of my own mind, on top of the physical confinement.

The brief lulls were a coping mechanism — the survivalist part of me keeping me sane, despite the odds. However, soon the dismal questions would once again bubble to the surface.

How was I going to escape?

Would I even get a chance to escape?

Were Nya and Sherrine really alive?

Were this ogre and his tribe going to tear me limb from limb?

Would I even survive this night?

When my brain was mercifully at rest, I didn't have to debate these urgent questions back and forth with myself over and over again.

I took a deep breath and enjoyed the small moment of stillness.

My quiet reverie was suddenly broken by the screeching of bolts being dragged across the door, which abruptly swung open.

The door's movement was so quick that it slammed into the back of the concrete wall, reverberating loudly before ricocheting backward at speed, almost hitting Myrah in the face as she entered the cell.

I was disappointed when she was able to stop the door with her foot. For a moment I fantasized about it hitting her with enough force to make her drop the tray of soup she was carrying — the hot liquid spilling onto her tunic and searing her flesh. But then again, I wanted the soup.

I made no effort to stand up when she approached me. I kept myself cradled in a tiny ball, guardedly staring at her as she wandered slowly across the small room.

"Here's your dinner, bitch," she said acidly, slamming the tray down on the floor with such violence that some of the soup sloshed out of the bowl and on to the tray.

I craned my neck and inspected it, then glared up at her.

"It doesn't look much like dinner to me," I said.

"Be grateful you're getting anything at all…you dumb cunt," she countered.

I clicked my tongue and shook my head disapprovingly. "Such language out of a Senior Sister. As a higher up, you should be closer to God."

"I *am* a Senior Sister, and you are wise not to forget that," Myrah declared, defensively.

"I'm sorry to hear that, as are all the sisters," I quipped.

Myrah tightened her jaw. She looked like she was ready to breathe fire. I gave her an indifferent look, gloating inside because I was able to get a rise out of her.

Myrah reached for the tray. "Fine, I'll take it back upstairs. When Vitora gets wind of the fact you are wasting food, she'll come down here and lash you to death."

I smirked at her. "How do you expect to trade me to an ogre if I'm dead?"

Infuriated, Myrah reached her hand back and smacked it down with brute force onto the side of my cheek. I gasped and drew my hands up to my stinging face. The pain burned through my flesh, scorching me with fury.

I stood up and reeled my hand back, slapping Myrah hard in the face for the second time in one day. Consequences be damned! She was *not* going to treat me this way.

"Don't you *ever* lay a hand on me again," I growled through clenched teeth.

Myrah's blood-shot eyes glared at me with hatred.

"You are a detestable animal. You are *exactly* where you belong…locked up in a dungeon," she spat. "And soon, you'll get *exactly* what you deserve. To be fucked to death by a gang of filthy ogres."

My blood rushing, I adopted a fighting stance.

Despite my being weak from a lack of proper food, Myrah could sense that my burning anger had given me renewed strength and resolve. She didn't rate her chances in the face of my fury.

She spun on a heel and quickly marched towards the door. When she got to it, she bent down and picked something up that was sitting in the hallway.

Myrah carried a silver pail back into the cell with her. She set it down a few feet away from me — out of striking distance. It was filled with water and had a brown sponge floating on top. She placed a small fragment of soap next to the pail.

"Wash yourself thoroughly, so you'll be presentable for the ogre when he returns for you tomorrow," she commanded, with an angry huff.

I came forward and dipped my index finger into the water. It was frigid.

"It's ice cold," I said, glaring up at her.

Now it was Myrah's turn to give me a smug smile of satisfaction. "Oh well. That's your problem. Have fun, bitch."

She practically skipped out of the room with glee, closing the cell door and locking it behind her.

I didn't want to eat the soup. It was the principle of the matter. But I was starving and I knew that if I wanted even a slim chance of escaping, I had to fuel my body whenever I was given the opportunity.

The soup was watered down and barely had any vegetables or meat in it. It was lukewarm at best, but I resolved to finish every last drop of it.

I glanced at the bucket of cold water that I was supposed to use to wash myself. The water was not only cold, but horridly murky.

It looked like it was dirty dish water rather than drawn freshly from the tap. Knowing Myrah, I was sure that this was her personal touch to amplify the humiliation. At least she had the human decency to provide a piece of soap, although it was miniscule.

A short while after Myrah left, the viewing hatch of my cell door opened with a clang. A pair of pale green eyes revealed themselves through the gap. They were curiously scanning the room through the narrow hatch.

A moment later, the door swung open again.

Sister Elisse charged into the room with an angry scowl on her face. Her cheeks were flushed but her chestnut hair was sleek and groomed, making me envious that, as a woman, I had lost the luxury of any femininity whatsoever. While physical appearance wasn't supposed to mean much to a nun, I'd nonetheless always been quietly proud of my golden hair.

Elisse stopped directly in front of me. As quick as lightning, she swung her arm out and knocked the bowl of soup from my hand. I had barely taken my first mouthful.

The tepid liquid spilled everywhere, all over me, all over the floor.

It was in my hair, on my face, in my lap. My mouth was agape with pure shock as I stared at Elisse with utter bafflement.

"What did you do *that* for?" I protested.

I wanted to punch the sneer right off Elisse's face.

"Myrah told me about how you treated her when she graciously brought you the soup."

"Glad to see you have so much free time to sit around and gossip with each other," I said, dryly. "Hope I can make it as a Senior Sister one day, sounds pretty cushy — apart from having to lick Vitora's scrawny backside."

Elisse's upper lip twitched. "Filth like you doesn't deserve to be fed."

"Nice act…keep it up," I chastised. "The new girl will do anything to prove she's a vicious Senior Sister. If that's what you really aspire to be, then I pity you."

"*You* are the one who should be pitied," Elisse said.

"I'm locked in a dungeon," I shrugged. "I'm not the one torturing people. Doling out misery and suffering is not the way I make myself feel good about myself."

I was aiming to make her feel guilty, but she wasn't taking the bait. She kicked at the bucket of grimy water. A little sloshed out over the sides.

"You better begin washing yourself, you filthy animal," she said, looking disgusted.

"How original," I rolled my eyes. "Calling me the same name as your hero, Myrah."

"You have bugs in your hair, how else can I describe you?" Elisse contested, crossing her arms over her chest and cutting me an accusatory scowl.

"How is that *my* fault?" I scoffed, sardonically.

"Here is the bucket," Elisse said, kicking it again. "There is no reason for you to be dirty if you *use* it."

She was speaking to me like I was a child.

I pointed to the water. "This water is dirtier than *I* am."

"I don't care," Elisse said, her lips twitching again. "You have soap. Wash yourself…or else."

Or else what, I almost barked back, but I didn't want to argue with her all night, so I opted to hold my tongue.

I could only push these Senior Sisters so far before they reached their breaking point and snapped on me. Elisse was an unknown quantity, and I didn't know how far the depths of her vindictiveness reached. I had to figure out where the invisible line was, and not cross it unless I absolutely had to.

"Clean up for the ogre," Elisse ordered, once she realized she wasn't going to be challenged. "He wants you in pristine condition, and he'll be here tomorrow to pick you up. You need to satisfy his expectations."

The sheer audacity of the request loosened my tongue once more.

"Of course — let me jump right to cleaning myself up," I said, wryly. "Better not disappoint the repulsive monster and his rapist horde. I want to look presentable for my murderous fuck fest."

Elisse took a deep breath, as if she was trying to summon patience. She closed her eyes and whispered something inaudible under her breath.

When she opened her eyes, she locked them with mine, then spoke slowly and deliberately.

"If you aren't clean when he returns for you, then the ogre will take another sister from the convent — one that is more 'presentable', as you put. Either way, he is leaving with a nun tomorrow, that is the agreement in place. I'll let the responsibility for that sink in with you."

Elisse spun abruptly on her heel, her loose hair whipping behind her as she moved swiftly towards the door.

"Goodnight Sister Elisse," I called out behind her. "I shall pray for your eternal soul."

The door slammed shut.

The silence was deafening.

I was left with my roiling thoughts.

Elisse was right, no matter how much it pained me to admit the fact.

If I didn't comply with the command to clean up for the ogre, then the beast wouldn't hesitate to take another innocent sister.

Having met the vile creature, I had little doubt that he would leave with a nun slung over his giant shoulder tomorrow, come what may.

I couldn't live with that on my conscience. I had taken the vows to protect my sworn sisters. My decision was instant — but it didn't make it any easier to bear. I had no other choice but to sacrifice myself.

My chin began to tremble. Hot tears stung my eyes. I hated to cry. It was a sign of weakness, but I was so distraught and bitterly sad that the tears flowed involuntarily.

I choked back most of the sobs, but my shoulders shook. I was unable to physically suppress my grief.

I thought about Sister Geneville, wishing she was still alive. How I longed for her tender consolation and compassionate touch. She was everything that a Mother Superior was meant to be.

Reluctantly, I stripped off my clothes. The chill instantly surged through my bones once my tunic was removed. I cried as I rinsed myself with the sponge and the dirty, frigid water.

Tears rolled down my cheeks as I rinsed my hair. The muddy water spilled down my back, taking my breath away with its freezing touch. I scrubbed my skin until there wasn't any dirt or grime remaining.

I hadn't been provided with a towel of any kind, so I had to use my own tunic to pat myself dry. The cheap, scratchy material felt harsh against my soft skin.

After I had finished drying off, I put the damp tunic back on and retreated to my usual corner of the cell, where I once again tucked myself into a little ball in an attempt to preserve heat.

My stomach rumbled with hunger. Stabs of grumbling pain

sliced through my gut. I was ravenous. For a moment I even contemplated licking up the soup from the floor, but I couldn't bring myself to do it. That would make me the animal Elisse and Myrah condemned me as.

I was exhausted, both emotionally and physically. I closed my eyes, desperate to find sleep. The faster I succumbed to unconsciousness, the faster I could remove myself from the brutality of my situation.

"For my sisters…" I whispered, chanting the words over and over again, muttering the incantation under my breath until my throat hurt. "For my sisters…. for my sisters… for my sisters…. for my sisters…"

My final despairing thought before sleep claimed me was that, for the first time in my life, I didn't care if I never woke up again.

Chapter Three

It was meant to be the happiest day of your life.

I was dressed in a white lace gown, with a mesh veil covering my face. The dress looked ornate but, on closer inspection, you could see the frayed stitches and tatty hemline. The used garment was the best my parents could afford on their meagre income as farm laborers.

The landowner — Garadain was his name — had always taken a keen interest in me, even when I was a small child and my parents took me to their work, as there was nowhere else to leave me.

Garadain, a huge, rotund man with a protruding belly and several chins, allowed me to stay in the main house while my mother and father toiled in his fields. I was given the leftovers from his own children's meals. My parents were grateful for his 'generosity'. Only I knew that his charity came with a price — one I could never reveal, as it would cost my parents their livelihoods.

With his own wife long dead, Garadain asked for my hand when he thought the time was appropriate — I was twelve. My parents felt they had little choice, as their income depended on the landowner, and they knew I would not go without. "You could do a lot worst," was the most enthusiastic recommendation they could muster.

So there I sat on the ornate bed, draped in a tatty wedding dress and looking down at my hands. Garadain, flushed in the face from alcohol and anticipation, lifted my veil, then slowly brought his face closer to mine. But something was different this time.

As he approached, his face started changing. His ears grew pointy tips. His red, bulbous nose morphed into a brutish snout. His grey eyes darkened to a bottomless black. Drool began to slobber from the sides of his mouth and drip down his chin.

Closer and closer he came. Our faces were only an inch apart now.

He let out a detestable, animalistic grunt before grabbing the back of my head with a giant, calloused hand. He held me in place as he opened his mouth and snaked out an unnaturally long, scabbed tongue. It was covered in warts and puss, his breath smelled like rotting carcasses.

He brushed his disgusting tongue against my tightly-sealed lips. I tried to squirm away, but his giant hand held me firmly in place. He slowly forced his coarse tongue between my soft lips and then...

Loud screeching jolted me awake.

I sucked in a sharp breath and my arms involuntarily flailed away from my body, trying to repel the shape-shifting monster.

My muddled mind was unsure of where I was.

The screeching sound bore into my very soul.

My eyes flew open and I took in my dismal surroundings.

My heart sank — I had left one nightmare only to re-enter another.

I stirred, rubbed my eyes with my fingers, and stretched my sore, aching muscles.

A chill surged up and down my spine — due to the frigid cold of the room but also the shadowy tendrils of the nightmare that were still wrapped around my consciousness.

It was the same recurring dream about my childhood, but this time with a monstrous twist.

However, it slowly and horrifically dawned on me that the awful final scene of my nightmare could actually become a reality for me very soon.

The screeching noise mercifully came to an end as the bolts were fully retracted.

The door abruptly swung open.

Elisse charged into the room with a determined look in her luminescent green eyes. Her features were steely and focused.

I was still unnerved by my disturbing dream, but didn't want to reveal my unease. So I attempted to use sarcasm to mask my unsteady emotions.

"I love to see a fresh face first thing in the morning," I carped.

Elisse gave me a salty glower. "I wish I could say the same thing about *you* but—"

She cut herself off and halted in her tracks, pausing to shoot me an astonished glance. Her eyes trailed me from head to toe.

"What?" I said, finally shaking off the nightmare and regaining my bearings. "Are you surprised that the 'animal' cleans up well?"

"You do look…presentable…" she trailed off, continuing to stare at me wide-eyed.

"Does that mean we can finally be together?" I chided.

Elisse wrinkled her nose with distaste. "Hardly."

She rapidly motioned for me to stand.

"Get up," she ordered, when I remained on the floor.

I slowly rose to my feet, standing tall to face Elisse.

There was a brief silence between me and the Senior Sister. Our eyes were locked on each other. I was sizing her up, trying to determine how much of a threat she really was. I think she was doing the same with me.

I decided to opt for a less confrontational strategy.

"You don't have to do this, sister," I said, my tone gentle.

"What?" she replied, somewhat taken aback.

"This is not you, Elisse," I continued, more urgently.

While there were only the two of us present, I might have a chance.

"You're not like Myrah or Vitora," I continued. "You are not *evil*, just misguided and…lost, sister."

Her eyes widened.

I wanted to see if there were any remnants of human decency left within Elisse, but was abruptly interrupted when booming footsteps bellowed down the hallway. They stopped directly in front of my cell.

The door crashed open again.

I froze as Vitora walked in. Her menacing dragon whip was cradled adoringly in her bony fingers as her slender frame sauntered into the room with a determined swagger. She had her usual cruel and snide expression on her face.

Stepping in behind her was Myrah, taller in stature than Vitora, followed by the heavy-footed ogre, who was simply monstrous in size.

Myrah's eyes widened in shock when she saw me — perhaps due to my transformation — but I felt there was something deeper there.

The lumbering ogre was scowling, until he laid eyes on me. Then his dirty, saggy features seemed to light up.

He looked at me with ravenous infatuation. "This is the same bitch from yesterday?"

He pointed at me and blinked, having to do a double take.

Vitora clapped her hands together proudly. Her lips curled into a saccharine smile, but I saw the darkness residing deep in her irises.

"Yes she is, the very same," Vitora declared pompously, as if she was responsible for cleaning me up like a shiny new penny. "Isn't she a picture of cleanliness?"

"I'm fresh, but am I monster-rape-death fresh?" I grumbled sardonically under my breath.

The ogre grunted and stared at me with a confused glance, wiping the drool dribbling down his chin with an enormous dirt-stained hand. He smacked his lips as he eyed me greedily.

I hated the depraved way he stared at me. It made me shudder with revulsion and foreboding.

"What did the bitch just say?" He swiveled to address Vitora.

Vitora chuckled lightly and waved her hand dismissively. "Who knows, and who cares. The cunt — and her cunt — are pristine, as promised. Do with her as your will compels you, honored protector."

She cut me a lecturing glare and leaned in closer to me. "Shut the *fuck* up and don't ruin this for us," she warned under her breath, with a threatening hiss. "Remember your sisters."

I swallowed hard and stared at the floor. The ogre was so revolting that it made my stomach queasy just to look at him.

Elisse stepped forward.

"I came in early to make sure Hana was ready and presentable, dear Mother," she declared. "All is as it should be, I am pleased to say."

I rolled my eyes. So Elisse was simply trying to impress Vitora with her work ethic. It seemed she was beyond redemption after all. The corruption had spread too far within her.

Vitora smiled beatifically. "I'm pleased that you took the initiative, Elisse." She cast the Senior Sister a slight, yet formal bow of approval. "Good work, indeed."

It gave me a small measure of satisfaction to see Myrah frown at the praise given to her peer — and no doubt rival. She quickly turned to face Vitora.

"I made sure she was provided with the water and soap," she interjected, a little pathetically, as if she was competing for the affection of a stern parent.

"Freezing cold, dirty dishwater," I spat.

The words charged out of my mouth without thought or restraint. It seemed that a part of me had accepted my grim fate, so speaking out of turn no longer worried me. In fact, it was the least of my worries.

Myrah shrugged, her lips curling into a cruel half-smile. "It got the job done, didn't it? I mean…you're still *ugly* in my opinion, but you can't fix ugly with a bucket of water and a bar of soap."

"Very wise words, sister," I said. "Judging by the look of you."

Myrah gave me a furious glower. Her upper lip twitched in protest, but she didn't say anything further.

Vitora glared at me viciously, her eyes forming into narrow slits of derision.

"I'm sure your smart mouth will be put to good use by our honored guest and his noble tribe for their sport," she said. "I'm tempted to place a wager myself. What are the odds being offered?"

"I'd say the odds of you going to Hell for all eternity are one hundred percent," I countered.

At this point, what did I have to lose? They were going to turn me over to this murderous beast no matter what, there was no escape.

Perhaps a part of me wanted to trigger Vitora's fury, so she would lash me to death with her whip there and then, and thus spare me the prolonged torture I had in store at the hands of the ogre and his village of savages.

My mind was all over the place. I needed to recalibrate.

I could not win my freedom now, but that didn't mean an opportunity would not present itself in the near future. For the time being I was stuck with this ogre, no matter what.

My sisters, I reminded myself. I had to ensure that I was the one taken and I did not place any other nun in mortal jeopardy.

I noticed out of the corner of my eye that Myrah was once again giving me a fixated look. She was taller than both Vitora and Elisse, lanky and awkward.

"Can I help you?" I said curtly, turning to face her.

Myrah cleared her throat, snapped herself out of her seeming daze and shifted her weight with unease. She gave Vitora a sheepish glance, then scrambled for a suitable cutting response.

"You can help me by accompanying the nice ogre and dying a horrifically painful death," she said with contempt. "In fact, after she's dead, why don't you keep her corpse as your own private fuck doll," she suggested to the ogre. "She'll be usable for a good few days before she begins rotting."

A glazed look came over the ogre's dark eyes. I could almost see the gears turning in his small brain — he was actually contemplating it.

"Shall we complete the transaction?" Vitora snapped, clearly impatient.

Transaction? It was as if I was a gleaming coin ready to be

handed over for services rendered, rather than a sister of the holy order under Vitora's supposed motherly protection.

I glared at her. "I am a human being."

"Not for much longer," the ogre countered, then slapped his thigh with glee, impressed at his own 'witty' retort. His coal eyes flickered hungrily. It appeared he was starved for excitement, and I was to be his entertainment of choice.

I instinctively took a step backward, but Myrah quickly positioned herself behind me to stop me from getting very far.

She coiled her cold hands tightly around my upper arms and shoved me forward, towards the ogre.

"Where do you think *you* are going?" Myrah taunted, with a sickening laugh. "This is a one-way journey for you, in every sense."

The ogre began to chortle along with her. The cacophonous din of their cackles flooded through my ears. Both had eager expressions on their faces, their mouths wide with amusement.

"*Enough,* Myrah," Vitora snapped. She was clearly impatient for this to be over with, yet she dared not offend the ogre.

"The bitch is all yours," she said to the beast.

"I'm going to give her a good look over first," the ogre grumbled, stepping closer to me.

He sniffed greedily with his grotesque snout as he approached, towering over me. He smelled like dirt, rotting flesh and feces all mixed together. I held my breath and looked down. The tufts of patchy hair on his bare toes were so nauseating that I had to look back up again — drool began to leak from his twisted lips.

The two openings in his snout flared wider as he sniffed me deeper, all the while walking in a slow circle around me. He lifted my hair and brushed his sausage-like fingers through it. I winced at the touch, it was so repulsive.

I got a good look at his gritty fingernails. They were caked with dirt, as were his fingers, hands and arms. In fact, his entire body was matted in thick grime. At first I thought he had a naturally dark complexion. But at this close proximity I realized it was in fact accumulated filth coating his skin. He looked like he had rolled around in mud just before arriving at the convent.

The ogre lifted my tunic. I whimpered and froze, paralyzed with fear. Was he going to try to fuck me right here, in front of the other nuns?

He glanced at my backside, then craned his neck around to leer at my crotch. His eyes were wild with excitement. His foamy drool began to slop to the stone floor. He finally put the garment back down and nodded curtly at Vitora.

"She is acceptable," he declared.

Vitora's shoulders relaxed and she released a deep breath.

"The Lord is merciful and kind, granting us the gift of agreement," she proclaimed, then pressed her hands together and raised her head to the ceiling, murmuring an incantation under her breath.

"You are a sick woman," I told her. "God sees your sadistic crimes. You will reap ten-fold what you have sown."

Vitora reeled the handle of the whip back and struck me across the face with it. The impact was jarring and made me wobble. I saw stars and was dizzy for what seemed like a full minute.

"My parting gift to you, *cunt*," she said, almost gleefully. "Give our ogre friends a decent showing before you perish, take *some* pride in your duties."

She nodded at Myrah, who pushed me out of the room and into the corridor.

The ogre followed us out, then roughly planted his hands on either side of my hips and heaved me over his shoulder like I was nothing more than a sack of feathers. This close, his stench was overwhelming. I retched, but there was nothing in my belly to expel.

My fate was sealed. I was powerless to stop it. But I still flailed and kicked at the monster in a vain attempt to win my freedom — it was an instinctive reaction. I dug my nails deep into its drooping, weathered skin. He didn't even seem to notice.

He trundled off towards the basement steps with me bouncing up and down on his saggy, rancid flesh. This high up from the ground, I felt a wave of nausea, almost like being seasick.

"You will stand in judgement for your sins," I cried, my voice echoing down the hallway. I tried to squirm out of the ogre's grasp in an effort to secure my freedom, but his giant hand pinned me firmly in place.

I closed my eyes and offered a silent prayer to the Savior. It seemed Divine intervention was my only hope now.

Chapter Four

The ogre kept me slung over its colossal shoulder for the entire trip back to its home.

My arms hung limply at my sides, too fatigued to fight anymore.

I had flailed, punched and kicked until my limbs were numb, but the ogre didn't even flinch. It was like a moth trying to take on a rhino. Hopeless. The ogre's grip on me was like an iron claw.

I stared at the ground as the ogre whisked me away with its giant strides.

Its large, intimidating shadow bobbed along behind it. I stared at the morphing silhouette, stretching and changing its angle as the sun slowly dipped lower in the sky.

From my vantage point, I observed the terrain changing texture as we continued on the journey, from soft grass to gravel to dirt, then hard scrabble and uneven rock.

The ogre's physical presence — its grime and dirt-caked arms, its foul-smelling armpits and saggy, leathery flesh —

brought sour bile to the back of my throat.

The overpowering stench and nausea-inducing up and down motion was too much for my already heightened senses. I had to escape — in spirit, at least.

I went off to another place in my mind, using prayer. It was the only coping mechanism available to me, for now. If I didn't pray through my apprehension and despair, then the fear would consume me, of that I had little doubt.

I prayed soundlessly, mentally, privately.

As a nun, this ability to lose oneself internally and block out external stimuli was one of the best resources we had to cope with trying circumstances. I had used it extensively when I first entered the convent and found the restrictive and austere life of a nun overwhelming.

I silently recited the short Deliverance Canticle — taught to me by my beloved mentor, Sister Geneville.

From darkness to light, my soul shall be lifted from despair and danger. From darkness to light, my soul shall be lifted from despair and danger. From darkness to light, my soul shall be lifted from despair and danger...

The rhythm of the incantation was accompanied by the repetitive sound of the ogre's bare feet shuffling through the underbrush we now found ourselves traversing. The regularity of the two sounds lulled my mind into blessed calmness. For a blissful while there were no external thoughts crashing into my consciousness.

My quiet reverie was interrupted, however, when the ogre suddenly stopped dead in his tracks.

I stiffened, going on full alert. My eyes flew open and I saw he was stood atop hard rock.

"What's going on?" I asked, not really expecting an answer

from my captor.

It was unseasonably chilly. My breath plumed in front of my face as I spoke.

I tried to wiggle to readjust myself. It was atrociously uncomfortable being hiked over the beast's shoulder. Mercifully, he slackened his grip and I was able to stretch my back a little.

"We've reached my dwelling place," the ogre grunted, irritably.

I lifted my torso and looked around as far as I could turn my head.

I didn't know *what* I was expecting to see, but I certainly wasn't expecting the surroundings before me.

I blinked and stared at an uneven row of large caves with hollow, black openings. The caves were etched into a massive stone valley. There was no greenery or vegetation anywhere, just unforgiving, cold rock as far as I could see. God only knew what lurked behind those ominous dark entrances.

"This…this is where you live?" I asked, mentally cursing myself for the unmistakable cadence of fear in my voice.

The ogre chuckled, sourly. "Is it not to the prim and proper bitch's liking?"

I tightened my jaw. "I just…it's—"

"As if I fucking care, *bitch*," he interjected, gruffly. "You are here for our entertainment, *not* to receive our hospitality."

"That much is clear," I muttered, wanly, under my breath.

The ogre was on the move again, trudging towards the last, largest cave on the outer rim of the cluster. We passed a raised area where the ground was unusually flat and even.

The caves were set in a deep granite valley, no doubt carved by the sea hundreds of years ago. The walls of rock seemed to block out any ambient sounds from the environment.

If not for the appalling circumstances I found myself in, I might have even described the atmosphere as serene.

That was until the ogre stepped foot inside the cave.

The setting was abominable.

A pungent smell of death and decay instantly slammed into my nostrils, making me retch. The cave reeked of decomposition, rot, sweat, urine and excrement mixed together to form an indescribably abhorrent odor. The floor was made of mud and dirt. That explained why the ogre was covered in a thick layer of grime from head to toe.

Filth was littered everywhere. Half-eaten animal carcasses lay picked apart and sprawled out on the floor; the preys' dead, glassy eyes stared up pitifully. Piles of excrement sat in the corners of the dwelling, covered with angry flies. Maggots were writhing around on the dead animals, enjoying a rich and putrid feast. I reached my hand up and plugged my nose, yet the vile stench still managed to flood my senses.

The ogre didn't make any effort to set me down, for which I was thankful. Given the fact that I was barefoot, I didn't want to touch any part of the filthy ground with my body. For once, I was actually relieved to be hoisted on the beast's broad, uncomfortable shoulder.

He carefully retreated to a far corner, picked up what looked like a large animal horn, and exited the cave again. He walked to the raised area we passed earlier and stepped up onto the flat expanse of rock. I saw a length of thick rope on the ground before us, one end of which was wrapped several times around a large boulder. Panic rose in my chest.

The ogre roughly placed me down and immediately grabbed the ankle of my left leg, so I had no chance to run. He knelt down and wrapped the rope around my ankle, using his considerable strength to form a tight knot. Satisfied I had no chance of escape, he stood back up.

He took a deep breath and lifted the smaller end of the animal horn to his mouth. He exhaled sharply. The horn released a high-pitched sound that pierced through the valley, amplified by the ricocheting echoes from the stone walls.

I stood up, on high alert, my breathing intensifying and my heart racing.

Morbid thoughts of my impending death began to flood my mind.

The ogre breathed in deeply again, releasing his breath into the horn once more. It rang out for the second time.

This time, he got the response he was looking for.

One by one, other ugly, menacing, towering ogres began to shamble out of their respective caves, blinking into the light of the day.

Noticing me and my captor on the raised area, they began congregating in a large circle around us, scratching the tops of their scruffy heads, blinking at us with increasing curiosity.

I was so petrified that I couldn't breathe as I looked out onto the group of monsters. My throat felt like it was closing in on itself.

The ogres were equally as tall and equally as detestable as one who had brought me here. They were burly, wearing vulgar expressions of excitement, lust and anticipation.

It didn't take me long to realize that the ogre standing next to me was the leader of this particular tribe of savages. He threw the horn down and addressed his comrades. His voice was deep and carried like a rumble of low thunder through the crowd.

"The first payment has been made by the God-woman," the

ogre explained to the excited throng. "That payment is the human bitch you see in front of you. LET THE GAMES BEGIN!" he roared with jubilation, holding his arms aloft and balling his hands into tight fists.

A deafening eruption of cheers rang out.

The ogres all raised their arms in the same gesture as their leader.

"As promised, you will all get your chance to take the bitch," he continued. "In *whichever* manner you wish, but you'll have to wait until tomorrow," he warned, sternly.

Murmurs of disappointment grumbled through the air.

The chief ogre raised its brutish hand to silence the complaints.

"You need to exercise patience, brothers. Tonight we open the book and wagers will be placed as to how long she will survive. Once the coin has been tallied, you will have your fun tomorrow."

I swallowed hard, crippled by anxiety.

"She doesn't look like she'll last long," shouted one of the ogres at the front, a look of disgust plastered on its ugly, brutish face as it scanned my body. "How do we all get our chance?"

"Trust me, you shall *all* get your turn, come what may," assured the leader.

I didn't even want to begin to contemplate what that meant.

"Every last comrade will get their fill — or, should I say, fill the bitch," he chuckled loudly, admiring his own crass witticism. "So pick your hole — pussy, ass or mouth — it's all for the taking."

More animalistic whoops spewed loudly from the crowd.

I couldn't believe what I was hearing. Tomorrow they would be impaling me with their monstrous cocks until every last one of them had deposited their vile seed deep into my ass, pussy or down my throat.

I willed myself not to cry, even though hot tears burned my eyes. My chances of survival were dwindling down to nothing. The realization was like a punch to the gut. My knees buckled and I wilted, falling to the hard, stone floor.

"Get up, bitch. Stand, so they can get a good look at you," the ogre hissed at me, angrily.

"No." I shouted, mustering what little remaining courage I had left, and looked him square in the eyes.

The ogre took a clump of my hair in its mammoth hand and aggressively pulled me upward. I yelped as pain seared through my scalp. I had no choice but to get to my feet, lest my hair be ripped from its roots.

"She's a feisty one, I'll give her that, and doesn't care to mind her manners," the ogre chuckled to its brethren. "Take that in account when placing your bets — she's got a bit of fight in her."

"She's gonna have a bit of me in her, soon," another ogre yelled, gleefully.

More eager cheering and clamoring stirred the crowd.

They all moved forward, as if possessed. They wanted their fill of me, eager for a taste. Their desire to have me in every bestial way and then tear me limb from limb shook me to my core.

How did I get to this place in my life? What went so wrong that everything has spiraled out of control, and now I faced the most excruciatingly horrific death imaginable?

I took a look around at the growing legion of ogres. Their greedy expressions revolted me. They pressed in on each other to get closer. I trembled as their leader took a step towards me. Then, in one swift movement, he ripped my tunic from my body.

"Take a good look at the meat," he bellowed. "View her carefully before you make your bets."

Another odious cheer went up.

I stood there naked and petrified. I roped my arms protectively over my chest, but the ogre spitefully yanked them apart and held them at my sides.

"Have yourselves a *good* look," he encouraged.

The ogres began to step even closer, forming a narrower circle around us.

I was panting hard, engulfed by debilitating panic. The horde's lust-crazed expressions bore into me. My heart hammered inside my chest.

There is no way out of this. I am going to die at the hands of these wretched beasts.

I turned to my teachings and remembered that my physical form was nothing more than a loan from the Divine, that it was my soul which was precious and everlasting, but it did little to assuage my despair.

At least I would have one final night of prayer to prepare my soul for departure from the physical realm. It was my last chance to make peace with the Creator, my last night alive, my final bodily experience.

Thinking of my body, I instinctively attempted to cover my flesh again.

"Keep your hands *down*, bitch," the lead ogre warned with a murderous leer.

"I'm *cold*," I said.

I clenched my jaw shut to halt my chattering teeth.

"Does it look like I give a *shit* about your comfort, bitch?"

the ogre said, spraying drool from its mouth.

"I have a name. It's Hana," I spat back.

Of course, it was a ridiculous thing to say to a monster hell-bent on rape and murder. What consequence was my name? But I wanted him to know that I was a real person with a soul, with a life history, with an identity, not just a piece of meat.

"And my name is Tyrankreg-Gimtulan," the ogre said. "Be sure to scream it out loud when I'm fucking you tomorrow," he added, slapping his knee as he chortled. His nostrils flared grotesquely and a bit of snot leaked out as he snorted.

Meanwhile, I could see thick drool dripping from the assembled ogres' mouths as they eyed me hungrily with deranged expressions on their ugly, saggy-skinned faces. Their hollow black eyes cut right through me.

Once their leader had recovered from his self-induced hysterics, he cuffed his cold, rough hands over my hips and spun me around. He then spread my feet apart before pushing my head lower, so my back was arched and my rear was sticking out.

"This is what you will be getting," it praised. "Look at that inviting ass; you are in for a treat tomorrow, indeed. Make your choice — which hole do you want to fill?"

"Do we *have* to wait until the morning?" one ogre whined impatiently, stepping forward.

I turned around to see who it was.

Horrifyingly, the ugly brute lifted its black loin cloth and pulled out its cock, which was erect and pointing like a steel beam towards the sky. It was absolutely colossal and thicker than my arm. The ogre opened its mouth to reveal a mangled row of blackened stumps and sneered at me through its coal-black eyes, all the while stoking the monstrosity between its legs.

I gasped as shock and horror cascaded through me.

I wanted to run. I wanted to bolt, but I couldn't. My leg was tied firmly with the rope. There was no escape.

A bitter wind whipped through the air, chilling my flesh.

"I'm cold," I said again, turning my head to glare at the chief ogre.

"Why should I give a fuck?" The brute turned to give me an indifferent scowl.

His black eyes were menacing. His nasty mouth was twisted and caked with a combination of dirt, drool and snot.

"They've seen me in the nude. They can place their wagers with that knowledge," I said, giving the ogre a pleading look.

He simply ignored me.

The other ogres began creeping closer still, shuffling forward, narrowing the gap between us. The mob clustered in a full circle around me, inspecting every inch of my exposed flesh.

Their hungry faces disgusted me. Their slobbering mouths and devious grins sent a chill down my spine.

One by one, they began to pull their enormous cocks from the black fabric covering their groin regions. After the first one had exposed himself, it seemed that they all wanted in on the vile display. These were animals with not an iota of shame.

They were doing it to pleasure themselves but also to show me what I had in store for me tomorrow — hundreds of gargantuan cocks impaling me relentlessly, one after the other.

Warm tears spilled down my cheeks, but I kept a stoic expression on my face and stared ahead with my head held up. I was broken, yes, but I was still alive, and life meant there was hope, no matter how miniscule.

The ogres surrounding me began to grunt and moan as they slipped their grimy, stubby fingers around their bulging shafts and began stroking. None of them took their eyes off me, not once. Their starving expressions and the foamy drool running down their faces and slopping onto their chests made me want to retch. It became appallingly apparent that they were feeding off my distress.

"Your suffering makes me so hard," an ogre at the front shouted, excitedly. He was taller in stature than some of the others, with wiry black hair atop his head. His loin covering was discarded on the floor next to him and he had his swollen, veiny cock in his hand. I could see pre-cum glistening on the tip of his shaft as he worked it urgently.

"The pain is going to bring you exquisite pleasure tomorrow," he said, horrifyingly. "Turn your tears on for me when I fuck you, it's such a thrill to see you cry."

These beasts had no morals, no shame. They had zero qualms about stroking their thick cocks out in the open as they ogled at me. Their disgusting drool was now sliding off their bare chests, falling and wetting their hairy, monstrous feet.

I scanned the horde of lust-crazed ogres standing before me with their huge members out. My breathing intensified. My pulse drummed through my ears. I didn't want to look at their ugly faces, but I was horrifyingly transfixed by their huge throbbing rods, which were being pumped in meaty, animated fists. I placed a hand on my pussy in an attempt to hide it.

"Hands down," the ogre ordered, aggressively. I complied and placed my hands by my sides.

There I stood, on full display for an army of primal savages who would soon have me in every beastly way. The ogres looked like a pack of hungry wolves, ready to devour me in seconds — which they no doubt would have done already, if it were not for the strict instructions from their chief.

I felt like I was skirting the edge of a panic attack. My throat felt swollen. The world was spinning. My gut was churning in a sea of unrest.

From darkness to light, my soul shall be lifted from despair and danger. From darkness to light, my soul shall be lifted from despair and danger. From darkness to light, my soul shall be lifted from despair and danger...

I chanted the Deliverance Canticle in my mind to bring myself some solace in the face of fear. The ogres didn't have free agency over my thoughts. I still held dominion inside my own mind. I was not completely defeated — yet.

The lead ogre turned back towards me. Tyrankreg-Gimtulan — his name came back to me.

He grunted and leered at me, but he was not touching himself, unlike the others. He seemed to be the only one with a modicum of self-control.

His bushy eyebrows furrowed as he looked out onto the sea of ogres, his eyes narrowed with concern and distrust.

"The bitch will be guarded tonight," he announced. "In case any of you have ideas. The meat must remain untainted until the wagers are tallied and the new dawn breaks."

Grumbles of disappointment hummed through the air.

It was abundantly clear that many of them had been planning to ignore the rules and give in to their bestial lust right away, making short work of me.

"The guard will be Grimkerag-Triegrut," the lead ogre announced.

More groans from the crowd.

A mammoth ogre began shuffling towards the raised area where I was held captive. He was at least a full head and shoulders taller than any of the others. He was so remarkably large and hefty that his footsteps boomed as he shambled forwards awkwardly, trying to balance his colossal weight. His arms were too long for his body. They swung haphazardly at his sides, nearly touching the ground.

In his right hand was a mammoth wooden club with sharp metal spikes protruding from the bulbous end. The other ogres cut him a wide berth as he walked up to the raised area and gracelessly heaved himself onto the flat plain.

As he approached, I could see the skin around his elbows was caked with dirt and loose, sagging halfway down his forearms. He too had the tell-tale black eyes, which stared directly at me with a steely intensity. Mercifully, his loin covering remained wrapped around his mid-section. I couldn't even imagine what it would be like to be taken by this shambling behemoth.

"This is Grimkerag-Triegrut," the chief ogre informed me.

"Pleased to meet you, sir," I replied, dryly.

What was I expected to say?

Despite my derisive tone, inside I was falling apart. I felt like if someone tapped me, I would shatter like glass.

I sized up Grimkerag-Triegrut, craning my neck up to take in his full enormity. He had a horrifying presence. The lethal spiked club in his hand did little to soften the impact. The bridge of his nose was crooked and his top lip curved unnaturally upwards, giving his face a deformed appearance.

"You will be safe this one night," said the chief ogre, surprisingly moderate in his tone now. "Make peace with your maker."

"I have to stay out here all night?" I asked.

"Where else do you expect us to put you?" the ogre grumbled, then turned to face the crowd once again, raising his voice to be heard above the babble.

"Go back to your caves. The show is over — at least for today."

Grumbles of disappointment hummed through the air.

"You aren't getting her tonight, so wipe that idea from your minds right now," he continued. "Just in case your cock overrules your head, Grimkerag-Trigrut here will show you what he has to say about it."

The giant ogre let out an aggressive grunt.

There were a few more murmurs of discontent, but the horde appeared resigned.

"Go on, then," the chief ogre instructed, more firmly, pointing back to the cave entrances. "Get out of here. Go home. Get some rest. You will need your energy for tomorrow."

One by one, the ogres began to slink off, vanishing back from where they came.

I sat on the cold, stone floor, still naked and shivering. I wrapped my arms tightly around my body.

In a surprising final act of mercy, the chief ogre picked up my tunic and tossed it to me before walking away to his own filthy hovel. I snatched up the garment and quickly put it on. It was torn but, given the circumstances, I wasn't complaining one bit.

I looked up at my giant bodyguard. He simply stood there like an immovable mountain, brooding. His dark eyes were staring fixedly at me, his fearsome weapon clutched tightly in his grip.

Remembering my convent incarceration, I curled myself into a small ball to try to preserve what heat I could. I closed my eyes to block out the world around me.

From darkness to light, my soul shall be lifted from despair and danger. From darkness to light, my soul shall be lifted from despair and danger. . .

Chapter Five

I jolted awake and took a sharp intake of breath.

For a moment I had no idea where I was. But the dull ache in my body from where I was lying against hard rock brought harsh reality flooding back.

I lifted my head.

A bright moon was high in the sky and a blanket of darkness canopied the stone valley.

I moved my left leg — it was still tied securely with the thick rope.

The rope was coarse, rubbing the flesh of my ankle raw. I tried not to move or readjust myself very often, but while sleeping I had no conscious control of my movement. Now every time I moved my left leg, excruciating pain burned a ring around my ankle.

I was uncomfortable and exposed out in the open. My bed was a cold slab of unforgiving rock and the cold wind served as my blanket, caressing my body with its frigid tendrils.

I was too afraid to close my eyes now. Before, sleep had

claimed me without resistance. But now I was on high alert. I wouldn't allow myself to succumb again.

The crowd of brutes had dispersed, scattering back into their revolting caves. They seemed to understand that they couldn't fuck the literal life out of me until tomorrow. But I wouldn't put it past any of the depraved creatures to try their luck tonight. Guard or no guard, blood and lust befuddle the brain.

I had already resigned myself to the fact that I wouldn't live to see another sunrise, so I resolved to enjoy this one — my very last — and thank God for the miracle of creation as new light flooded the world. I had carried my cross my entire life, and now it was time to gently place it down. My time was over yet, paradoxically, so was my suffering.

I looked towards the horizon, where the first shimmers of His light would soon brighten the dark and foreboding sky. Then I turned my head to stare at Grimkerag-Triegrut.

He was sitting upright on the stone, his giant legs sprawled out in front of him. He looked distracted as he cradled his fearsome spiked club in his hands.

I noticed a few flies were buzzing around a flesh wound on his calf. It looked like a superficial injury. The cut wasn't very deep, but the area was red and swollen. There was some white puss oozing out of the sides.

I sat up and turned to him, remembering my sworn oaths as a nun.

"You'll get maggots in that wound if you don't clean it," I said and nudged my chin towards his leg.

The ogre turned his head slowly and stared at me with confusion.

"What, cunt?"

So he could speak. I hadn't been sure before. However, his words came out slurred due to the deformation of his upper lip.

"Your leg injury. It's going to get infected. It's not severe right now, but it could get a lot worse, especially if your dwelling is not…tidy." I struggled to find the right diplomatic word.

Grimkerag-Triegrut studied me with a frown. At this close proximity I saw that he had a pronounced overbite, which exposed a top row of brownish, decaying teeth inside his wide mouth. Large amounts of drool dripped down his chin and collar bone from where he could not close his mouth snugly. The overbite meant a gap would always remain. I actually felt a little sorry for him.

"Mind your business, cunt," was the curt, but clear, reply from the guard.

I sighed deeply and raised my head to the Heavens.

"I tried," I muttered under my breath, before lowering my head again.

"Will you at least loosen the knot around my ankle?" I asked, hopefully. "It hurts badly."

The ogre laughed mockingly. "Nice try, cunt. What do you take me for?"

"I'm not asking you to free me," I pleaded, meaning what I said. "I want to kneel for prayer with the sunrise, so I can make my peace with the Lord. Kneeling will be more bearable if the knot is loosened, even just a little. Will you not spare me one final kindness on my last day alive?"

"You can kneel before my cock," he replied. "I'm happy for you to worship that."

His face suddenly became animated as he eyed me ravenously.

Sickened, I lay down and tucked my knees up to my chest in a protective ball.

"Why don't you give me a little taste of the goods?" Grimkerag-Triegrut teased, with a mischievous smirk on his gross, wadded lips. "Pay me back for protecting you out here."

"You're a monster," I said, glaring at him.

"What's the harm?" he shrugged, casually. "As you said, you are dying tomorrow, anyway. *You* should be sparing *me* one final kindness on your last day, cunt."

A lump formed in my throat. My pulse began racing. I was tethered with the rope — there was no running, no hiding. I stared at the ground, tracing a crack in the stone with my finger to preoccupy my swirling thoughts.

"It's not fair," the ogre sulked, like a spoiled child. "I do all the work out here in the cold, but they all get a taste. It's not right, not right at all."

He stood.

I immediately bolted to my feet, moving as far away from him as the rope would allow. The coarse fibers tore at my ankle, sending sharp waves of pain up my leg.

"Your leader said *no one* can touch me until tomorrow," I hissed.

I lifted my gaze and stared directly into the colossal beast's eyes. "That includes *you*."

After a contemplative pause, he ripped off his loin covering and took his hard cock in his hand. It was the biggest I'd ever seen, easily as large as my leg. If that thing was going inside me, then there would be no 'me' to speak of very soon after.

I could have kicked myself. I had spent the whole evening on alert for danger coming from the caves. Yet here was my supposed guardian and protector turning on me viciously.

I should have known better. Honor, integrity and duty meant nothing to these monsters.

Trapped due to the rope, I could not flee. I could not fight. I only had my words.

"Your chief, Tyrankreg-Gimtulan, he will—

"Fuck him," spat the ogre. "No one can stand before me. Tyrankreg-Gimtulan should have allowed me a taste, that's all I ask for, a taste."

With his gargantuan cock in one hand and the menacing club in the other, he closed in on me, beastly depravity flickering in his black irises. He licked his lips with devilish hunger as he narrowed the gap between us.

I tried to back away, but the rope was at full extension. Searing pain was my only reward.

The ogre was right in front of me now, towering high above. He reached out a hand towards my neck.

I stiffened and opened my mouth to scream…

Suddenly, two shadows flashed in front of me. They were smaller in stature than the ogre, but still huge by human standards.

The scream in my throat was suppressed, replaced by sheer astonishment.

I glanced up and realized that the newcomers had jumped down from natural ledges formed in the rock above us. They hadn't made the slightest sound, and were now locked in fierce combat with the naked Grimkerag-Triegrut.

My wide eyes took in the action unfolding in front of me.

I realized from their distinctive appearance that the fighters were orcs, dressed in leather battle armor covered with spiky tusks — on their helmets, wrists and shoulder plates.

While the ogre was far bigger and mightier than his foes, the orcs had the advantage of stealth and speed. They also had the element of surprise, having caught the ogre completely off guard.

The orcs wielded spiked balls on chains, which were attached to wooden handles held firmly in their grip. They swung the weapons with dangerous precision, never once hitting each other or themselves as the spiked balls whizzed through the air in all directions. These were obviously highly-trained and skilled warriors. They worked in practiced co-ordination to land blow after blow on the heavy-footed ogre.

Why they were attacking the ogre, I had no idea.

The sound of grunts and shuffling movement filled the night air.

Arms and legs swung, flailed and shifted as the orcs worked tirelessly to bring the brutish ogre crashing to the ground.

However, Grimkerag-Triegrut was simply immense and wouldn't go down without a fight.

He raised his spiked club and swung it in a wide arc through the air. The speed of its movement was astonishing as it whistled through the air.

The cruel spikes made contact with one of the orcs — horrifically, directly in the face. I gasped in horror as the orc crumpled to the ground, clutching at its ripped cheek and nose.

The other orc, seeing that its partner was down, started swinging his weapon at the ogre's knees in an attempt to destabilize the behemoth and bring him down.

Over and over he swung the ball, which crashed into Grimkerag-Triegrut's thick legs with jarring thuds. Crimson blood ran freely.

The tactic appeared to be working.

The ogre swayed on its feet as it sought desperately to stabilize its balance. It lifted its club in both hands and swung savagely for the head of its attacker. I could tell that if the blow made contact, it was unlikely that the orc would have a head to speak off.

At the very last second the orc fell to his knees, managing to duck out of the way of the whizzing club. The gruesome weapon swung just inches above the orc's head.

The momentum of the club sent the ogre, who was already teetering on battered knees, spinning off balance. He lurched forward clumsily and then fell heavily to the ground. Dirt plumed around him.

He tried to get right back up, but his immense bulk and the fact that his knees had sustained damage meant he was struggling.

The orc wasted no time in seizing the opportunity. He sprang to his feet and charged towards the thrashing ogre.

His comrade, still clutching his now blood-stained face with one hand, joined the attack. Despite his own suffering, he instinctively knew that this was their best chance, so he needed to join the fray.

Together, they rained down blow after blow on the flailing ogre.

I didn't know what the orcs wanted with me — or even if they were here for me at all. But any fate was better than certain death at the hands of the savage ogres. I remembered that Nya and Sherrine had sided with orcs, but I had no way of knowing if these ones were aligned with them.

As the orcs continued raining down blows with all their might, I could see that Grimkerag-Triegrut was struggling.

His movements became slower and more labored. He made no attempt to swing his club now, which was held limply in an unmoving hand.

His gangly extremities went limp. He let out one last heave of breath. Blood pooled in his mouth and dribbled down his chin. His mouth was agape. I could see his cold, lifeless, black eyes were wide with shock.

Satisfied that the deed was done, the ogres fell to their knees and heaved in big lungfulls of air to recover from the exertion.

The unhurt one lifted his eyes to mine, then got to his feet and approached me.

He pulled out a short dagger from his belt then looked at me.

My heart jumped into my throat. Was this to be my end? All this, just to die?

"Do not fear, my name is Vakar. I am not here to hurt you," he reassured, urgently.

He bent down and began cutting the thick rope around my ankle.

The wounded orc got to his feet, still clutching his face and wincing in agony. Blood poured from underneath his hand, where his face had been sliced open by the ogre's vicious spikes.

With a final slash of the knife, the rope around my ankle was shorn. I was free.

I let out a sob of relief.

"Shh," the one called Vakar said. "We have to get out of here." He turned to his wounded comrade.

"Kalun, brother, is it bad?" he asked, looking worried.

"I shall live," said the other orc, breathing heavily.

"*Dinshaluk-Mohrical*" replied Vakar, in language I had no knowledge of.

"*Dinshaluk-Ephareem,*" replied the one named Kalun, a renewed strength in his voice as he uttered the strange words.

Then something completely unexpected happened.

Grimkerag-Triegrut let out a piercing death cry.

I wasn't sure if he had still been alive or his lungs were simply releasing the remaining pent-up air, but a high-pitched wailing sound escaped from his open mouth, before his chest fell for the final time. The shrill sound echoed through the cavernous stone valley.

A moment later, I heard voices coming from inside the caves, then the sound of motion.

"Come on," Vakar said, tugging my arm urgently. "We have to run, *now.*"

"Carry her," Kalun, instructed. "It will be faster."

I nodded to them both. "He's right. My legs are stiff from being immobile for so long."

Sunrise had begun and faint light was slowly creeping into the world. That would make us visible — and vulnerable. We had to make haste.

Vakar scooped me up into his powerful arms and whisked me away as fast as he could carry me, with Kalun right behind us, still gripping his battered face.

I didn't know what these orcs wanted with me, but I had no reservations in leaving with them. They had freed me from certain death at the hands of Grimkerag-Triegrut; that was a promising start.

The orcs were far quicker on their feet than ogres and we traversed the slowly-brightening landscape at speed. We quickly left behind the cold stone of the ogre's lair and hit dirt-covered ground, before encountering underbrush and soft earth as we entered a dense forest.

Once we reached the belly of the forest, I received the shock of my life.

Standing in a clearing, wearing a cream-colored dress with tousled, chestnut hair and a broad smile was — Sister Nya! My God, it was really her. My heart burst with joy.

The orc placed me down on the ground gently.

"Nya?" I asked, elated and stunned.

She didn't say a word, just opened her arms with a beaming smile on her beautiful, delicate face. I ran to her, my arms outstretched. We embraced in a tight, emotional hug, both of us crying with a mixture of joy and relief.

She cupped my face in her hands and kissed my forehead tenderly, which brought back memories of my beloved Sister Geneville, making this moment even more poignant.

"My dearest Sister Hana," she said. "How wonderful it is to see your beautiful face again. I can now finally breathe again, knowing you are safe."

"My beloved sister," I replied. "*You* are the angel that has answered my prayers."

Nya reached for one of Vakar's hands. He had deep green eyes with a kind and noble warmth to them.

"This is Vakar," Nya said, introducing us.

Vakar reached out to shake my hand, but I embraced him in a hug instead. It was the only gesture fitting for what he had risked for me.

I could see that he and Nya were a couple by the way they held hands dotingly.

Behind us, Kalun took a sharp intake of breath. We all turned to look at him.

"Kalun!" Nya exclaimed and jogged over to him. "My God, what happened?"

He still clutched his wounded face but I noticed the blood was not flowing as freely as before. It must have congealed in an attempt to heal.

I exchanged a worried glance with Nya. "I saw it happen, it's pretty bad. There's a gaping wound."

"We need to hurry back to the village," said Vakar. "We cannot be sure we weren't followed, though we were quick. Let's get moving."

Nya nodded and looked at Kalun. "Can you make it?"

"Yes, it is only my face. I am otherwise unhurt," Kalun said.

I felt that was a brave understatement. His face was twisted in agony. He looked miserable.

We set off at a fast clip through the forest, with Vakar leading the way.

Despite his anguish, Kalun wanted to remain at the rear to enclose me and Nya in safety and also tackle any potential threats. He was exceptionally brave in my eyes. Everything that a warrior was meant to be.

I glanced at Nya as we jogged through the woods in the direction of the orc village.

So many thoughts were racing through my mind. I had to get them out.

"Why did you come for me? How did you even know where I was? Is Sherrine really alive." I tossed a cautious glance over my shoulder at Kalun. "I'm worried about him."

Nya seemed plagued by concern, and guilt, as well. "Me too, sister, but we couldn't have left you. The chance had to be taken. Kalun and Vakar, they understand the dangers. It's part of who they are."

I gave her a quizzical glance. "But why would you risk that for me?"

"You are the first, dear Hana," she said, with resolve. "We plan to free *every* sister. Each life is sacred. The tyranny cannot continue."

My eyes widened. So what Vitora had said was true.

"I'll explain more once we reach safety," Nya continued, breathing a little harder now from the exertion. "For now, we must keep moving. Danger looms near, and Kalun is in desperate need of treatment."

With my mind still full of questions, but my heart lifted, I put my head down and raced forward, safe in the company of my dear sister and the two heroic orc warriors.

Chapter Six

When the orc village finally came into view, I allowed myself to breathe a sigh of relief.

Even though this milestone brought fresh succor to my spirit, I was under no illusion that my journey had come to an end.

While I vowed to stay in the present moment, I couldn't help feeling deep in my bones that an invisible storm was brewing around us. All of us.

However, I was no longer in any imminent danger. For that I raised my head to the Heavens and delivered a silent benediction of gratitude.

The sky was domed with a silvery, pastel-lavender hue as the light of dawn began to erase the darkness. It was the perfect representation of my life in the past few hours.

I smiled, allowing the growing illumination to bathe my weary soul.

"From darkness to light—"

"...my soul shall be lifted from despair and danger," Nya finished for me, giving me a knowing smile.

"Never have truer words been spoken," I said.

"It's the same invocation that saw me through the worst storms," confessed Nya. "The Deliverance Canticle is close to my heart, too."

Right then, it hit home to me that Nya had been through the same torture under the terrifying reign of Vitora. She understood the atrocities of being locked in a cold, dark basement like an animal. We shared a common bond through our struggles. I knew when I confided in her, she would understand at the most visceral level what I was going through, because she too had endured torment and hopelessness. She was my sister in ways far beyond the oaths we'd taken at the convent.

I reached out and squeezed her hand, not having to utter a word.

We stepped out of the forest clearing and entered the perimeter of the village, Vakar still leading the way.

The setting was primitive and remote, but clean and bright — a world away from the squalor of the ogre lair. In fact, my initial impression was that the village was quaint and charming, homey, even.

Of course, *anything* was better than a dismal convent basement or a filth-infested ogre cave. A shudder ran down my spine at the bleak memories.

I scanned my surroundings as dawn rays bathed the landscape.

There were clusters of wooden structures dotted around a central square. The buildings appeared to be made from cedar wood. Some were obviously dwellings while others seemed to be used for storage, trading and crafts.

Vakar put his arm on Kalun's shoulder. The wounded

warrior was still clutching his ripped face.

"I'm going to take him to the healer, and then I will be home," Vakar told Nya, giving her cheek a tender stroke, which made my heart gallop.

Nya turned to Kalun.

"You were *so* brave today," she said, reaching out to clutch his giant hand in both of hers. "Your actions will not be forgotten."

"I owe you my life," I added, feeling terrible that he'd sustained his horrific injury because of me. "That is a debt I can never repay to you."

"It was both my duty and my honor," replied Kalun, the effort of speaking clearly causing him pain, yet he still took the trouble to assuage my guilt.

"Go now, I'll see you shortly," Nya said to Vakar, giving him a doting smile.

I was elated for Nya, seeing that she had found her place in the world and the love that she deserved a thousand times over.

It probably wasn't the path she had envisaged for herself, but it was becoming apparent that none of us could predict what life had in store for us.

"I can't wait to catch up with everything that's happened in your life," I said to Nya as we approached the cabin she shared with Vakar.

"I'll get you up to speed," Nya promised, cuffing her slender fingers around my hand as she tugged me eagerly along.

"I thought I heard voices out here," a female voice said.

A figure approached, emerging from the shadows thrown by the cabin.

In the glow of the new dawn, I saw her slender silhouette and made out long, cascading hair.

My heart leaped with joy.

"Oh my goodness," I exclaimed and placed a hand to my suddenly thumping chest. "Sherrine…Sister Sherrine?"

"Hana?" came the equally surprised voice.

Sherrine stepped fully into the light, a look of pure astonishment in her vivacious brown eyes.

Her honey-blonde hair was wavy and fell halfway down her back, longer than I remembered. She was wearing a white lace nightgown. She looked like an ethereal goddess.

Sherrine rushed towards me and roped her arms around my body, embracing me in a tight, warm hug. I buried my head in her shoulder as a tear escaped my eye and rolled down my cheek. Her hair smelled like cinnamon and spice.

While Nya had a delicate, elfin face, Sherrine was classically beautiful with high cheeks and full lips. But with both these unique women, it was their inner goodness and strength of character that made them truly radiant in my eyes.

I experienced a wave of contentment surge through my body. I felt like I was home, even though I had never stepped foot in this village before.

"Yes, it's me, dear sister," I said. "Nya, Vakar and Kalun bravely rescued me from the ogres."

"Ogres!" cried Sherrine, taking a step back and staring at me, her mouth wide open in shock.

"Yes," I said, wanly. "It's a long story. We have so much to catch up on."

"It's just so good to see you alive and well," Sherrine said, clutching both my hands in hers. "We have a long road ahead, but you are the first of many we will free from that atrocious convent."

I nodded encouragingly, but deep down I was worried. With

Vitora having enlisted the help of the ogres, I feared the orcs would be no match for their brute strength and viciousness.

I quickly pushed the thought to the back of my mind.

For now, I just wanted to relish being in the company of my lionhearted convent sisters, women who actually cared about me.

"I want to help in any way I can," I said to Sherrine. "I am with you in heart, mind and body."

She brushed her fingers through my blonde hair and gave me a sisterly smile. "All in good time, my love. For now, you must heal and recover."

Nya was beaming.

"Reunions like this give me such hope," she enthused. "This is just the beginning, sisters. We *will* free them all."

I took her hand and squeezed it, still holding Sherrine's with my other hand. "I am with you all the way, sisters, come what may. Your village is lovely, by the way."

Nya chuckled. "It's not luxurious but, as we all know, it's better than where we came from."

"Absolutely," I agreed.

A moment later, a tall, burly orc approached us. He had a deep olive complexion and was carrying a bouncing baby in his thick arms.

The baby's skin was a beautiful light green shade. He had curly, honey-colored hair just like Sherrine's, and two adorable pearly white teeth on both his top and bottom gums. He waved his chubby little arms animatedly and smiled with delight, squeaking "ma-ma…ma-ma" with glee upon seeing Sherrine.

I looked between Sherrine, the orc and the adorable baby.

Now it was my turn to hang my mouth open in surprise.

Sherrine nodded proudly and gently took the joyous baby

from the orc's huge arms.

She tousled the infant's bouncy curls and smiled at him with the loving affection that only a mother could project.

"This is my son, Armaan," Sherrine said.

I clamped my hands together, absolutely ecstatic. "Oh Sherrine, he is perfect."

Sherrine's features were aglow with pride.

"Thank you. He is a handful, but also a joy."

Sherrine gave a smile of affection to the enormous orc beside her. He looked older than both Vakar and Kalun, and was also a little larger in stature.

"This is Narag," she introduced.

I reached out to shake his hand. "It's a pleasure to meet you."

"And you, welcome to Sherrakh-Shen," Narag said, casting me a polite bow in greeting.

"That's the name of the village and this orc clan," Sherrine explained. "We live in that cabin," she added, pointed to a dwelling a little further along.

I let out a long breath and addressed all of them.

"I can't thank you enough for coming to my aid. I'd be dead right now otherwise, of that I am certain," I said, feeling overcome with gratitude.

Nya stroked my back delicately.

"We simply followed the righteous path, as we had been taught," she said. "We know what it's like to be a slave, to be a prisoner, to be sold."

Sherrine was nodding.

"We couldn't allow you to endure that same fate, Hana," added Nya. "Not you, and not any other sister."

"That's why we need to help the others as well," Sherrine said, her eyes shimmering with determination. "This abuse *has* to end."

I nodded. "I'll be with you every step of the way."

"If Hana has just come from the convent, she will have information that will be useful to us," said Narag.

The orc had a leader's bearing as well as an imposing, warrior's build. I could tell that he was much respected in the village.

"Why don't we go to my cabin," Sherrine suggested. "We were just cooking up some breakfast. We can talk while we eat."

My stomach rumbled with hunger. "I've never heard a better suggestion in all my life."

Sherrine glanced around and frowned.

"Where is Vakar?" she asked Nya.

"He took Kalun to the healer," Nya explained. "During the battle, he suffered a nasty wound to his face. Vakar will return after he ensures Kalun is being looked after."

Both Sherrine and Narag frowned with concern.

"It's not a life-threatening injury," added Nya. "Just a very painful and very visible one."

Somewhat relieved, the couple escorted us to their cabin.

Inside, there was a warm glow of apricot flames dancing in the hearth in the center of the main living area. The glowing fire spread its warmth throughout the entire cabin.

A lantern and candles illuminated the kitchen. Soon the smell of sausages and eggs in the pan wafted through my nostrils, making my mouth water.

Narag crouched by the fire to flip the sausages as Sherrine, Nya and I strolled into the kitchen and sat at the table.

"Narag is village head now," Nya mentioned. "Finally the orcs have a leader they deserve and can respect."

Sherrine's cheeks blushed rosy. "That's very kind of you to say, Nya."

"I heard that the previous chief was overthrown," I mentioned, remembering what Vitora had said back in the convent.

"Morgut." Nya said the name with disgust. "He is truly despicable and cruel. He is imprisoned and awaiting trial for attempting to murder little Armaan."

I gasped, wide-eyed with shock, staring at Sherrine.

"Unfortunately it's true," said Sherrine, instinctively scooping her little treasure into her arms. "But he's exactly where he belongs now."

Vakar stepped through the front door and came into the kitchen.

"There you are," he said. "I thought you might be here when I found our cabin empty."

Nya sat up straight. "Is everything okay with Kalun?"

Vakar nodded wearily and sat down at the table with us.

"He is in the hands of the healer now. He is getting the attention he needs."

"That's such a relief," Sherrine said and sighed.

Vakar nodded. "Indeed." Though he still seemed downcast.

"So…how did it all unfold," I asked, "To me, it seems like a Divine miracle that I am sitting here now with all of you."

Nya smiled. "It will probably sound simpler than it was to pull off."

Vakar concurred. "No truer words have been spoken."

"But it was worth it," Nya quickly reassured, reaching out her delicate hand to squeeze mine and giving me a loving smile.

"You know that we are making plans to free the sisters," she continued.

I nodded.

"Well Kalun, who is the head of guards, has, along with Vakar and I, been covertly watching the convent, trying to work out the best time to make our move, and also to see if Vitora has added any security measures. We mainly carry out our surveillance after dark, so we can approach closer to the building while remaining inconspicuous."

"But yesterday?" I said.

Vakar explained. "Yesterday we decided to keep watch earlier in the day from further out, in case we were missing any activity that wasn't taking place after dark. Narag, quite rightly, thought it was important to watch the convent at different times, so we had a more rounded view of its daily activities."

It occurred to me that Narag was a natural leader not only in terms of his manner and bearing, but also when it came to strategy and tactics.

"That's when we saw the ogre carrying *you* off in broad daylight," Nya said, her voice alarmed. "When I saw you slung over its shoulder, my heart stopped."

I was stunned by what I was hearing.

"So you just happened to be watching the convent earlier than usual yesterday, and spotted me being taken?" I asked, incredulous.

"Yes, and thank God we were there," Nya said.

"Thank Narag; it was his strategic thinking that ensured we were in the right place at the right time," said Vakar.

"Think nothing of it," said Narag, somewhat abashed, sizzling pan still in hand.

"I dread to think what would have happened if we missed you," said Nya.

She was not alone in that thought.

Nya was interrupted by baby Armaan, who reached beside

her and cuffed his chubby little fingers around her hand and squeezed it. With his free hand, he began to slap his palm against the table leg, cackling and babbling, proudly showing off those little pearly-white teeth.

"Armaan has stolen our hearts," Nya said in a love-struck voice.

"As he should…he's just *beautiful*. Bravo, job well done, Sherrine," I said, admiring the cute little fellow.

Sherrine was smiling wide. "Thank you." She grabbed his rattle from the table and took it to him. He reached out for it wide-eyed and then shook it with glee, babbling "rata…rata…" before looking at us all in turn for reactions as the toy filled the air with shooshing sounds.

Sherrine kissed the top of his head, picked him up, then returned to her seat.

"Sorry, we got a little off track there," she said.

Nya chuckled. Her cheeks were rosy. She looked so much healthier and happier than the last time I'd seen her. I hoped that, in time, the same would prove true for me.

"It's fine," Nya said. "I don't mind if Armaan takes the spotlight. He can entertain me all day."

"He does make the energy of the room brighter," I agreed, smiling.

It was almost as if Armaan knew exactly what we were saying, because he began to cackle and clap his hands together jubilantly. His bright brown eyes sparkled with vibrancy.

"We followed the ogre at a distance until he reached the caves," continued Vakar. "We positioned ourselves on a ledge overlooking the valley."

"We heard everything," said Nya, anger now entering her voice. "Their…*intentions* for you. It was beyond depraved, beyond evil."

She didn't have to tell me.

"We waited for the right opportunity for our ambush," Vakar continued. "Ideally, we hoped the big guard would drift off for a nap but, when we saw he was about to attack you, we had no choice, me and Kalun had to make our move."

A shudder ran down my spine at the terrifying memory of the ghastly Grimkerag-Triegrut.

Then my heart went out to poor Kalun. I offered up a silent prayer for him.

"We told Nya to retreat back to the forest, both for her safety, and so, if we did not return, she could inform Narag of what happened. We were not about to let that monstrosity rip you apart," Vakar said, tightening his chiseled jaw.

"We were with you every step of the way," Nya said, giving me a tender smile as she reached across the table to gently squeeze my hand again. "You were never alone, even though you must have felt it in your heart."

"Thank you. I owe you my life. I don't know how I can ever repay you," I said, overcome.

"You don't need to worry about that," Nya said. "Seeing you alive and well is all the repayment we need."

"Amen, sister," chimed Sherrine. "I'll make us some tea," she added, getting up.

"I can hold the baby for you if you like," I offered.

Sherrine smiled. "That would be wonderful, thank you."

She handed Armaan over and I cradled him in my arms. He looked up and gave me an adorable smile while shaking his rattle. I leaned forward and drew in a deep sniff of his little baby head. It was a truly lovely scent. I gently ran my fingers through his hair. His curls were exquisitely soft.

"I think my womb just did a somersault," I said, unguardedly. Everyone laughed.

Nya beamed before continuing her explanation.

"I was worried sick while waiting in the forest clearing, but I was also confident that Vakar and Kalun could get the job done and bring you back to safety."

"They are my best guards," added Narag. "You were in safe hands."

Vakar nodded at his chief humbly.

"Their courage is the reason I'm sitting here in this warm room right now, getting breakfast served to me instead of being ripped apart at the hands of those beasts," I said.

I was once again enveloped by a swell of gratitude as Narag handed me a plate with eggs, sausage and a type of seeded bread on it. Sherrine handed me a piping hot mug of tea. It looked like elderberry and had petals floating on the top.

I began to salivate with hunger. I was ravenous. I hadn't enjoyed a meal this opulent in a long time. I couldn't wait to dive in and devour all of it.

"I had hoped we could get away quickly and unseen after dispatching the ogre," said Vakar. "I wasn't expecting that scream just before he succumbed. It alerted the other ogres."

Narag sat down and looked intensely at Vakar. "Were you seen?"

"It was still dark, as dawn had yet to break fully, so I am confident that we fled before the other ogres could make out that we were orcs," said Vakar. "But I cannot guarantee we were not observed."

Narag sat back and contemplated, while drumming his fingers on the table.

Little Armaan began copying his father, making us all smile.

"I hope you are correct, brother," Narag said. "But we cannot discount the possibility that the ogres know it was us that stole Hana and killed their guard."

"It *was* dark," Nya said, by way of reassurance. "By the time they reached me, the landscape was still shrouded mostly in shadows. I don't think they could have made out the details of Vakar or Kalun."

"Yes, that is the hope," said Narag, before tuning to me. "Hana, I am sorry if this is a difficult subject for you, but we must know what is happening at the convent and how the ogres are involved."

"Not at all," I replied. "I've been waiting to tell you what I know."

"But eat first," Narag said, kindly. "While the food is hot."

He didn't need to tell me twice. I tried to maintain some decorum but, in truth, I devoured the delicious food and warm, spicy tea with abandon. Little Armaan was still in my lap and I fed him some of the egg, which he slurped down with a gurgle of glee. It was pure heaven.

Satiated, I looked up at the little group.

I coiled my hands around the still warm mug. The cute baby bounced and jiggled on my lap, happily shaking his rattle. However, my mood shifted to a more somber tone.

"What is it?" Nya furrowed her eyebrows with concern.

I licked my lips apprehensively and took a deep breath. "Vitora...she knows that you are planning to free the sisters."

"How?" Sherrine said with a gasp. Her cheeks went ashen with shock.

"Morgut; he still has orcs loyal to him among you," I informed, regretfully. "It seems not all are happy that he has lost power."

"I am not surprised Morgut has sympathizers in the village," said Narag, thoughtfully. "Not all orcs are willing to embrace peace and reconciliation. Our warrior heritage runs deep, and learning to co-exist rather than pillaging and taking forcefully will not happen overnight. But the question is, how much of a threat is this faction?"

"I wouldn't say much," said Vakar, dismissively. "Seeing as their evil bastard of a leader is rotting behind bars, where he belongs."

"Um…*language* in front of the baby," Sherrine lightly reprimanded.

Vakar's features creased with guilt. "Right. Sorry."

"There's more," I said. "And this is where the ogres come in."

Everyone leaned forward in anticipation.

"Vitora has made a deal with them to protect the convent in exchange for one nun a month for their sadistic pleasure. I was the first…offering."

"That's sickening," Sherrine said, wrinkling her face with disgust.

Narag squared his posture. His muscles bulged. "Sickening indeed. However, ogre involvement raises the stakes. It adds dangers and obstacles we were not expecting."

"What will it mean?" I asked, but I already knew the answer was going to be bleak.

Vakar met my gaze with a rueful expression. "It means our rescue plan is suddenly a lot more complicated and treacherous."

This, of course, was exactly what I suspected, but hearing Vakar verbalize it hit home hard.

"We can take down an ogre — as long as we have at least two orcs doing it," Vakar explained. "The one me and Kalun defeated was huge, but we took him off-guard. If they are prepared for battle, it will be that much more difficult, and it will be tough to take down a large cluster of them at once."

The food suddenly felt heavy in my stomach.

"Ogres are vicious, strong and not easily defeated," Narag agreed. "This is a most unwelcome development."

"Vitora's evil and cunning knows no bounds," I said, hanging my head,

Armaan turned around and touched my cheek affectionately. He looked at me as if he wanted to nurture and comfort me, instead of the other way around. Bless him. He was immensely intuitive, empathetic and concerned about others, much like his mother.

I roped my arms around his tiny body and embraced him in a hug as he patted my face some more. It was impossible to wallow in negativity when Armaan was around.

However, I still felt like a cloud had suddenly descended over us all, and no amount of cuddling with precious Armaan would completely subdue the storm thrashing inside me.

"What do we do now?" I asked, scanning the table hopefully.

There was only silence as everyone contemplated the weighty new information I had imparted.

After a few moments Sherrine walked over and cupped her hand over my shoulder.

"For now, you need to rest," she said, gently.

"Sherrine is right," said Narag, kindly. "You have been through so much already. Rest your body and your mind, Hana. You have been of great help."

That was easier said than done, unfortunately.

"You can stay with us," Nya offered.

"That's very kind of you," I replied.

Sherrine chuckled. "Trust me, you have a lot to thank Nya for in this instance. Armaan is a cutie now, but when he's practicing his warrior cries in the middle of the night, that opinion doesn't last long."

"Never!" I admonished. "He is a cutie through and through."

"Besides, you need all the sleep you can get," Sherrine added in a more serious tone. "I'm sure you are exhausted."

I nodded. There was no denying that fact.

Nya smiled. "My couch will be much quieter."

I kissed Armaan goodbye and placed him gently on the ground. He went on all fours and crawled under the table back to his mother. There was something about his motion that made me pause. A thought was trying to come to the surface of my mind, but I was so tired that thinking clearly was a struggle. I gave up and embraced Sherrine in a tight hug before saying my goodbyes and walking with Nya to her cabin.

Vakar stayed behind to discuss strategy further with Narag.

"You seem *so* happy," I said to Nya as we walked into her cabin. "It brings joy to my heart. I can tell Vakar thinks the world of you."

"I love him," Nya confided. "He is wonderful to me, the bedrock and anchor I've been looking for since my mother passed. And I hope I offer him strength and support, too."

"There's no doubt," I said, as I lay down on the large seat in the living area.

"It's been a whirlwind," I admitted. "I'm still trying to absorb it all."

"Take all the time you need," Nya said, offering me a patient smile. "Rest your weary spirit now, sister. From darkness to light—"

"I have been lifted from despair and danger," I finished for her, as my heavy eyelids fluttered shut.

My final thought before slumber claimed me was how delighted I was for Nya and Sherrine. No two people in the world were more deserving of peace and happiness than these two warrior women.

Chapter Seven

I woke to the sound of voices.

"Good afternoon," said Nya, as she gently pushed my hair out of my eyes.

I sat up and blinked.

As my vision came into focus, I noticed Vakar, Sherrine and Narag also in the room, in hushed conversation.

"Oh my!" I exclaimed. "I didn't realize I was *that* tired."

"It is for the best," said Narag, turning to me. "The body has its own innate wisdom. It is always wise to follow its lead."

We were all sitting around the fire in the living room.

Nya seemed pleased to have the company and was making tea and apple muffins. The aroma of the apples baking with cinnamon was heavenly to my senses.

I stretched my limbs and went to the bathroom to freshen up and clean my face. Nya had given me a new set of clothes and it felt rejuvenating to put on a clean, untorn tunic.

I returned to the living area and sat on the floor alongside Sherrine, both of us basking in the hearth's warm glow.

The mood seemed livelier today, especially as baby Armaan was toddling around the room, entertaining us with his squeals of laughter and joy.

He would stop walking every now and then to look at us for a reaction. Each time, we would cheer and clap for him. He would bounce up and down and clap along with us, babbling "Ama…wok….Ama…wok.", his rosy cheeks spread into a fantastic grin of pride.

As the fire crackled and we sat around sipping tea, I glanced around the room.

Everyone now seemed lost in their own little world, contemplating how we could win the convent sisters' freedom without suffering a huge loss of life at the hands of the ogres.

I searched my own thoughts.

The memory of Armaan crawling underneath the table to his mother yesterday suddenly came back to me. My weary mind couldn't grasp its significance at the time but now, fully rested, its meaning hit me with full clarity.

I crossed my legs and cleared my throat to get the attention of everyone in the room.

Alerted by the sound, Armaan crawled over to my legs and lightly tapped his little palms on my shins.

"I think you're his new favorite," Sherrine declared.

I scooped up the baby, who cackled and seemed delighted to be held in my lap.

"And he is mine," I said and kissed the top of his little head, before glancing up at the others.

"I need to tell you all something…something I remembered after watching this little fellow crawling under the table yesterday," I said, running my hands through Armaan's soft curls.

"Really?" Sherrine eyed me with intrigue, leaning forward.

I nodded. "When I first entered the convent, Sister Geneville was my mentor. She took me under her wing as she saw I was struggling to adjust to life as a nun. She was already quite old by then and had spent most of her life in the convent. She knew its history, layout and quirks better than anyone. She revealed to me that there was a tunnel leading from the basement of the convent out to the woods nearby."

"Seriously?" Nya stared at me. Her brown eyes were wide with befuddlement. "I've never heard of that."

Sherrine exchanged an equally skeptical glance with Nya, shaking her head. "Me neither. Are you sure, Hana?"

"Yes," I maintained. "Sister Geneville explained it was originally constructed to allow nuns to flee in case of attack or persecution. When the convent was originally built, religion was viewed with skepticism and distrust, a volatile mix that often led to violence. However, as the years rolled on and people became more enlightened, the threat of persecution diminished. The entrance to the escape route was covered up by decree of one of the first Mother Superiors, lest any sisters use it to make a dash for freedom."

"I'm not sure, Hana," said Nya. "It sounds like an urban legend. We cannot build a plan based on the stories of an elderly nun, however benevolent and wise she was."

"I've seen it with my own eyes," I countered.

The room went quiet. All eyes were fixed on me.

"It was a fluke, really…the discovery, that is," I explained. "During my early years at the convent I was always being assigned to clean the basement. On one occasion, I bumped the mop into the bottom of a wall and a stone came loose. Curiosity got the better of me. I glanced over my shoulder to make sure no one was watching, then crouched down and moved the stones. I saw a gaping cavity beyond. I realized it was the tunnel Sister Geneville had told me about; it couldn't be anything else."

Nya was wide-eyed with curiosity, but it was Vakar who spoke.

"So if we can locate the exit in the woods, we can get into the convent without having to force our way through the main gate?" he asked.

"Well, in theory, yes," I replied.

Sherrine stared at me with wonderment. "And no one else knows about this?"

"Well, I can't say definitively whether Vitora knows it exists or not. However, I have the feeling that, if she does know it's there, it's not at the forefront of her mind right now," I said. "Because the stones were replaced, you wouldn't notice that it's there. Out sight, out of mind, as they say."

I held my breath, awaiting responses.

"So it's safe to say that not many nuns know about it?" Nya asked.

I shook my head. "I don't think many nuns *ever* knew about it. It was just a historic architectural quirk of the building that was never used for its intended purpose."

Vakar gave me a mischievous smirk. "If *you* knew about it, you should have fled that appalling place when you still had the chance."

I let out a deep breath, rocking little Armaan in my lap. He was subdued, seemingly lulled by the animated conversation taking place around him.

"To tell you the truth, it's existence went completely out of my mind also," I explained. "This little warrior crawling under the table yesterday was the only reason why it rose back to the surface of my mind. We have him to thank," I said, gently squeezing Armaan's chubby little cheeks.

Smiles cracked on faces all around, while Armaan reveled in the attention.

"Besides," I added. "Where would I have gone? How would I have survived? The convent was a grim and unforgiving place, but our sisters were kind, and it was the only family I knew."

Nya and Sherrine both nodded, knowingly.

"Could we *all* pass through the tunnel?" Narag quizzed, staring at me expectantly.

Ever the leader, he was steering the discussion back to practical matters.

"It was made for humans," I explained. "From memory, I'd say a person of average height could stand up in it, though they might have to stoop their head a little."

"And orcs?" asked Vakar.

I glanced down at baby Armaan, who was still sitting calmly and serenely in my lap.

"You could crawl through, I'm almost certain of it," I reassured. "It would be a tight squeeze for sure, but you *could* make it."

"And the ogres?" Narag asked the obvious next question.

"No, not possible," I declared, breathlessly. "Having had the displeasure of their company recently, I know beyond doubt that they would be too big to fit through. Humans, yes, orcs, just about, but ogres, no."

As we began discussing the tunnel idea in more detail, I noticed a more positive energy permeating the room. Even little Armaan could sense it, by the way he spontaneously clapped his little hands together.

"We might actually be able to pull this off," Narag said, his eyes ablaze with optimism. "We need to send a scout to locate the exit in the forest."

He was usually so stoic and indomitable. If *he* was moved to show enthusiasm, then the plan must have validity.

"I can't wait to overthrow Vitora and her evil cabal," Nya said, animatedly. "God forgive me for striking out against a holy site." She closed her eyes and lifted them to the Heavens, no doubt preemptively asking for absolution.

"You don't need to apologize," I said. "This *is* the righteous path. Vitora is awful and she is indoctrinating her minions, such as Sister Myrah and Sister Elisse, to spread the corruption. The darkness is growing in that convent and they will continue to ruin the lives of ordinary nuns — the ones they don't barter to the ogres for rape and murder first."

"Hana is right," Sherrine said, her face set and unyielding. "Vitora will never stop, unless she is stopped."

Vakar had been quiet for a while. He finally broke his silence.

"This is all encouraging," he said. "Better than anything we have drummed up so far. However, there is every possibility that there will be ogres guarding inside the convent as well as outside."

My heart suddenly plummeted. Of course, why would it be otherwise?

Narag straightened his posture. "If that does turn out to be the case, we will deal with the ogres as we encounter them," he said. "We cannot avoid danger in this mission, and we cannot avoid conflict. Our purpose here is to find the most effective strategy, but it is foolish to think this endeavor will be without cost."

The room was eerily quiet for a few moments.

Vakar broke the contemplative silence.

"This is what we are trained for, as guards," he said, with resolve. "It is the risk we accept."

"Indeed," replied Narag, adding *"Dinshaluk-Mohrical,"* while looking a Vakar.

Vakar placed a hand to his chest. *"Dinshaluk-Ephareem,"* he replied.

"It is done," Narag declared, with cast-iron resolve. "We shall raid the convent in two days' time."

My fellow sisters and I gasped collectivity.

"I realize that may seem too soon," said Narag. "But I can assure you it is better than giving the ogres more time to organize themselves and plant guard posts around the convent. If this Vitora is as vicious and cunning as her reputation alludes, she is going to waste no time in ensuring her building is heavily fortified with ogres."

I looked between Nya and Sherrine. They both wore dubious expressions. I felt compelled to interject.

"Narag is right," I said. "Vitora is diabolical, capable of anything. From what she said while I was imprisoned in the convent, I had the impression that she only very recently made the pact with the ogres. Remember, I was the first 'payment'. We need to act before they can properly organize or bring in reinforcements. Delaying may blow any chance we have of gaining the upper hand. We cannot beat the ogres in terms of numbers or brute strength, so it's imperative that we maintain any advantage."

Narag suddenly stood, an urgency in his posture.

"Tomorrow we make our preparations. Armor and weapons must be readied. The guards need to be put through their drills so they are battle-ready."

Sherrine scratched the top of her head and her features were etched with tension.

She gently took Armaan from my lap and hugged him tightly.

Everything was moving at speed now, but I had little doubt that Narag had chosen the right strategy. We simply couldn't allow the ogres to organize in numbers. The more of those savage beasts we had to deal with, the less chance we stood of achieving our objective, and the more blood we would have on our hands.

Narag turned to Vakar. "You will oversee the preparations in the village?"

Vakar stood to his full imposing height.

"You have my word, it shall be done," he promised, before looking at Nya and giving her a brief nod of reassurance.

Something dawned on me.

We were missing one, and wasn't this particular one the head of the guards? Shouldn't he be central to these preparations?

"Where is Kalun?" I asked. "Is he still with the healer?"

Vakar and Narag exchanged a cautious glance.

Narag was the one to respond.

"Kalun is finished with the healer and is now…resting…at home."

"How's his wound?" I asked, remembering the ghastly gash slashed across his face from the spike of the ogre's dreadful club.

"It has been stitched up," Vakar mentioned, simply.

"Is he faring well now?" I asked, suddenly overwhelmed with concern for the poor orc who had risked his life for me — when I was a total stranger to him.

Vakar let out a deep sigh. "The wound *is* healing, but the stitching was difficult to perform. He prefers to remain in his cabin for now."

I could sense that he was not being completely forthcoming with me.

Noticing my disquiet, Narag said, "Kalun is captain of our guards. He is a leader and takes that duty very seriously."

"He just needs some time," added Vakar, before giving Narag an apprehensive glance.

My heart went out to the brave and noble Kalun.

Sherrine and Narag took Armaan home while Vakar went out to make initial preparations for the raid. I was alone with Nya.

"Where does Kalun live?" I asked.

"He's in the last cabin before the forest on the other side of the main square," Nya advised.

"I want to visit him, to thank him for what he did for me and try to offer some solace," I said, resolved.

"It didn't sound like he was in the mood for social visits," Nya said, frowning.

"No matter, I must try," I replied. "The oaths, Nya. We cannot turn our faces away from those in distress."

"I know, sister," she conceded. "And no one holds the oaths closer to their heart than you."

"Is it safe for me to wander the village alone?" I asked.

Nya nodded. "Yes, as long as you don't stray too far away. I can walk down there with you if you'd like."

"That's not necessary," I said. "If you are busy with your own tasks."

"I'm never too busy for you, Hana," Nya said with kindness flickering in her eyes. "He might not see you, though."

"Then so be it," I said, feeling determined. "He risked his life for me and then sustained a life-changing injury. I do not want him to feel that he has been abandoned to his suffering, that he has to endure his burden alone."

***

Several minutes later, I was standing on the doorstep of Kalun's cabin.

Nya advised she needed to return to prepare dinner, but reminded me that as long as I stayed within the village and didn't wander off, I'd be safe travelling back unaccompanied.

I took a deep breath and rapped my knuckles against the wooden front door.

I heard movement inside, but the drapes were drawn, and no effort was made to answer the door.

"Kalun?" I called out gently. "It's…Hana…the nun you rescued from the ogre village. I…just want to talk to you for a few minutes."

After a few moments I heard a shuffling on the other side of the door.

"I do not want to see anyone right now," Kalun stated, a note of melancholy in his voice.

"You don't have to be worried about your appearance or any judgement from me," I reassured, sensing that this might be at the root of his apprehension. "I just wanted to thank you and let you know your bravery isn't being forgotten. I am counting my blessings with every breath I take."

"That is gratifying to hear, Hana," he replied. "However, you do not want to see me this way…trust me."

"That's *not* true," I countered. "It won't bother me in the slightest."

I meant it with all my heart.

The door didn't budge.

I decided to try another approach.

"If you don't wish to see me then I understand," I conceded. "However, I'd like to remain here and pray for your healing. I shall kneel on your step and pray until you have regained the courage to face the world."

I went down on my knees and clasped my hands together.

Yes, it was a little crafty of me, and I felt a pang of guilt, but I was adamant that he shouldn't be alone with his suffering.

I heard a long sigh on the other side of the door, then it opened just a crack. I could see one of Kalun's green eyes blinking at me with curiosity.

I stood up and gave him the friendliest smile I had to offer.

After looking beyond me to ensure that I was alone, Kalun very slowly opened the door.

As I stood there on the threshold, he slowly came into view. However, his face was covered with a massive, olive hand. He clearly felt self-conscious and ashamed.

In the gaps between his splayed fingers, I could make out parts of the cruel slash over his nose and cheek. It was still red and raw, and looked somewhat mangled due to the crude stitching. Without his helmet, Kalun's head was completely bald and smooth. He towered over me.

He wasn't wearing a shirt, as he was obviously not expecting company. Every inch of his massive body was carved with solid muscle. His abs were shredded and defined. I found him fascinating to look at, but tried not to gawk.

He wore the customary brown leather covering around his waist, but nothing else. His muscular thighs looked as wide as my entire body.

"May I come in?" I asked, gently.

Kalun took a moment to consider my request.

"If you must," he grunted, refusing to meet my gaze.

I stepped in and stood somewhat timidly at the entrance, waiting for Kalun to usher me in.

He quickly closed the door and mumbled for me to follow him inside to the living area.

He sat down in a large padded chair and collapsed his shoulders, looking defeated as he hung his head, steadfastly avoiding my gaze. His hand remained fixed over his face.

I took a seat next to him without being prompted. The room was dark because he had the drapes drawn, and there were very few candles lit around the sparse cabin.

"You don't need to hide away," I told him.

Kalun finally lifted his head to look at me, his hand still hovering over the damaged part of his face. From what I could see of his features, his expression was etched with sorrow.

"I am hideous now due to my wound," he confided. "I can no longer command the respect that I once did."

I was heartbroken for him. I could clearly hear the pain and shame in his voice.

I gently lifted my hand and touched his wrist.

Kalun flinched, not moving his hand. He stared down at his lap, looking stoically sad.

"Don't…" Kalun trailed off, his voice tinged with grief. "You should not see me this way. I know some humans view us as monsters. I now fear that my fellow orcs will see me the same way."

"You are *not* a monster," I countered. "The ogres who abducted me…who wanted to do atrocious things to me…

those are the real monsters. Not you. You don't need to feel humiliated by a…battle scar. It's an indelible reminder of your courage and bravery. It's a mark of who you are, Kalun."

He stood up abruptly and turned his back to me, shaking his head with doubt. His shoulders were broad, his torso and arms thick with solid muscle.

I stood up also. Though he towered over me, I knew I had nothing to fear from him.

"Come sit back down," I gently encouraged.

Kalun shook his head and kept his body turned away from me. His hand never once left his face, even though it was not visible to me.

"I think it is best if you leave, Hana," he said, dejectedly. "Though I appreciate the—"

"I don't want to leave until I know you are okay," I cut in.

"I *am* okay," Kalun said, unconvincingly. "The wound is already healing."

"Not just in body, Kalun," I said, gently. "Sometimes the scars that run the deepest and hurt the most cannot be seen."

I walked around to face him. I hooked my fingers around his elbow and gently tugged at his arm to coax him to lower his hand. It was a bold move, rude even, but I was placing my faith in my instincts.

Surprisingly, he didn't protest. Slowly, he took his hand away from his face and revealed the full extent of the injury.

I will not lie. Internally, I gasped at the horrific, angry slash that streaked across the bridge of his nose and most of his cheek. It had been stitched together crudely, the flesh twisting as it came together. His entire face was slightly contorted as a result. The wound would heal, but haphazardly, and he would never look even close to the same again.

The village healer might be adept with herbs, salves and other mainstays of tribal medicine, but when it came to surgical procedures, his skills appeared to be severely lacking. For once, I wished I was back in the convent, where I would have had access to my medical supplies and implements.

Exposed and anxious, Kalun searched my eyes for a response.

"I will not insult you with deception," I said, reaching out to hold his hand. "The injury is severe."

His face fell.

"However," I continued. "Looking at your face reminds me that I had goodness and righteousness on my side. Whether you believe me or not, you have the face of an angel — it cannot be otherwise, for you were the one to answer my prayers when I was in dire need."

Kalun sat down on the seat heavily, and his eyes fell to his lap once more.

"Beauty comes from within," I whispered, sitting next to him and stroking his muscular arm.

His skin was warm. It invigorated my senses to touch him. Kalun's eyes remained rooted to his lap, but there was a growing aliveness in his features as I continued to stroke him.

"You are beautiful," I said.

He looked up, then laughed loudly.

"I have been called many things in my life, but beautiful has certainly not been one of them, even before this disfiguration," he said.

I didn't miss a beat.

"I didn't say you *looked* beautiful. I said you *are* beautiful."

Astonishment crossed his features.

"What you did for me was remarkable, beyond the call of

your duty," I said, feeling a pang of yearning that ambushed me. It came out of nowhere and I certainly hadn't been expecting it.

I fed into the feeling and gripped his arm.

"You will *always* be someone exceptional to me."

A sliver of a smile began to crack at the corners of his mouth. I got the sneaking suspicion that my words were going some way to soothe him.

Kalun lifted his gaze and gave me a meaningful look of appreciation. I could feel his mood slowly emerging out of the dark well of despair.

"You are overly kind. I just did what I had to do," Kalun said with reserve.

Staring into his eyes was like looking at a kaleidoscope. His deep-green irises were flecked with orange and blue hues. His gaze was intoxicating. A rush of energy pulsed through my body.

The rhythm of my heart carried through my eardrums and my pulse quickened. My skin felt cold and warm at the same time, a novel sensation.

I was starting to feel invaded by his gaze, but not in a hostile way. It was as if he was somehow coaxing me out of myself, calling to feelings I had repressed for so long.

I was hypnotized by Kalun's stare. Regardless of how he looked superficially, I was connecting with a deeper part of him. His essence. His goodness. His…desire.

I could see a fire flaring behind those piercing green eyes of his.

Out of nowhere, I felt overcome with desire. It wasn't something I could explain — nor suppress.

I shocked myself when *I* was the one to make the first move.

I leaned in and gently kissed Kalun. These feelings, this energy within me, could no longer be contained.

It was like an unseen magnetic force was bringing us together.

As soon as my mouth made contact with his, I lost myself to the moment, and to the euphoria. Kalun tasted masculine, spicy, savory, ethereal. His breath was quick on my lips.

He responded by lightly brushing my mouth with his. The sensation was like rose petals grazing softly against my skin. Then he kissed me.

I closed my eyes and succumbed to the pleasure, promising myself that for once in my life I would live in the moment and allow myself to be swept away.

We kissed with fevered passion. The chemistry was undeniable. The more I fed into my natural instincts, the more I felt it lift my spirit.

In the back of my mind were my vows, but I just couldn't rob myself of the intensity of this connection, when it had felt like years since I'd enjoyed literally anything.

I shouldn't compare myself to my two resolute sisters, but if *they* could break free from the binding chains of their pasts, there wasn't any reason why I couldn't weave a similar pattern for my own life.

Finally free of the oppressive convent, my future was an open book.

Kalun began to sensually massage my tongue with his. It felt incredible. At the same time, he caressed my back and shoulders softly.

He was being ultra-gentle with me, probably more than he needed to be. I got the feeling that he was trying to rein in his desire, lest he came across as too aggressive.

I pulled away from him and stared deep into his alluring eyes, returning his sensual, desire-glazed look. "You aren't going to hurt me," I reassured.

Kalun nodded, pushing my hair back behind my shoulders.

"You said that beauty comes from within," he said, maintaining his intense eye contact.

"Yes?" I asked.

"You are beautiful inside and out, Hana," he said. "It is rare to encounter a soul such as yourself."

I gave him a warmhearted smile. "Thank you, that is very sweet of you to say."

Kalun gently cradled my head in his hands and leaned in, pulling me in for another sensational kiss that made me want to lose my mind. I became lost in passion with the sensual way he tenderly brushed his lips against mine.

I placed my palm to his chest, relishing the drumming of his strong heartbeat. He was warm and firm all over, perfectly sculpted.

I began to smell a hint of something that seemed to heighten my senses. It intensified my feelings for Kalun and made me feel intoxicated with yearning for his touch. The scent was so raw and earthy.

I looked at Kalun with a new set of eyes, unable to resist him in any capacity — mind, spirit…and especially body. I was fueled with an insatiable hunger. Judging by the charismatic flare in Kalun's eyes, he was also experiencing that raw magnetism, that urgent, ravenous surge of desire.

"What *is* that?" I asked. "It smells so…*wonderful.*"

It was fragrant, fresh, earthy, sweet and salty all at once, and instantly made me salivate. My mouth wasn't the only place where I could sense a new wetness.

"It is my mating scent," Kalun said. "When orcs are aroused, it begins to release from our skin."

Intrigued, I leaned in towards his neck and inhaled deeply. The heady scent filled my nostrils and fanned the flames of my desire.

"Wow," I said simply.

Kalun smiled. "The scent only intensifies feelings that you already have, and cannot make you do anything that you do not want to. But, at the same time, it can be quite effective in lowering inhibitions."

He wasn't kidding. I snaked my slender arms around Kalun's neck and pulled him closer.

His eyes were dazzling with desire. I recognized that burning inside myself, too.

Things began to get hot and heavy between us, with lips and tongues roaming everywhere. I was so turned on I could hardly see straight.

"I've...never done anything like this," I confessed, casting Kalun an apprehensive glance.

"It's okay, we don't have to do anything you aren't comfortable with—"

"Shh..." I trailed off and drew my finger up to his lips, giving him an enticing smile. "I want this, and I want you."

"You want me?" he asked, arching a curious, yet hopeful eyebrow.

"More than anything in the world," I whispered, my heart full to bursting. "But I just want you to know, I don't have much experience with this sort of thing."

"You don't need experience," Kalun said with a flicker of kindness in his eyes, cradling his arms around me. "All you need is a heart that is willing."

I smiled. "I have that in abundance."

He leaned in and once again locked his lips with mine, sending me into a tailspin of joy as he feverishly kissed me. I pressed myself to him. I was mesmerized by Kalun's body. He was massive and hard...*everywhere.*

He released me, then stood up and undressed. I found myself gawking at his stunning physique. He stood before me fully naked, carved like a mythical god that you might see in a child's storybook. He was packed from head to toe with hard, defined muscle. My eyes were instinctively drawn to his huge, thick cock, which stood erect like a steel beam, pointing at the Heavens.

My breath caught in my throat. I felt mesmerized.

Kalun studied me with concern. "Is everything alright?"

"Yes," I said, blinking hard and snapping myself out of my stupor. "It's just...you are...gorgeous. I'm sorry. I'm probably making a complete fool of myself right now, but I'm simply amazed at how incredible you are."

I meant every word of it. This wasn't about me trying to make him feel good about himself after his injury, or repaying him for saving my life. This was about me wanting this kind, noble, protective warrior with every fiber of my being.

Kalun had a fiery expression in his iridescent green eyes.

"Can I see you, too?" he asked, his eyes wide with anticipation.

I inhaled his sweet scent and fed into the longing permeating my body as I stood. However, a small part of me was still apprehensive.

Kalun roped his arms around my waist and pulled me close to him. He rubbed my back gently in circles before trailing his hands down and cupping my backside.

I took a deep breath, relishing the way he touched me sensually while holding me close.

"If you are not comfortable with anything, I don't want to pressure you into doing it," he said.

I smiled. "You are one of the kindest souls I have ever met."

When he talked to me in such a respectful and considerate manner, it made me want to give him anything he asked for. Who knew good manners could make a girl wet!

I took a step backwards and drew in a deep breath, preparing myself to disrobe in front of him. I then hitched my tunic above my head in one swift movement and tossed it onto one of the chairs.

I stood in front of him completely naked — exposed but excited.

A surge of adrenaline pumped through my veins. My nipples hardened and became perky and erect. My pussy was glistening with wetness.

Kalun eyed every inch of my body with wonder.

"I've never seen anyone so breathtaking," he declared, with an awestruck expression in his wide eyes.

He sat down on one of the chairs then took my hand and pulled me towards him. He then lifted me by the hips as if I was a bag of feathers and sat me down on him, so I was straddling his massive thighs while facing him.

His massive cock — bulging, veiny and swollen with arousal — was positioned directly in front of me.

It was a huge turn on to see him so hard. This close to his body, his earthy orc scent flooded my nostrils, ratcheting up my desire. My skin prickled with goose bumps.

Impulsively, I felt the urge — no, the need — to cuff my slender hands around his proud rod. I didn't know what I was doing, I just went with my instincts.

I held his throbbing cock in my hands. It was so thick that I had to use both hands to wrap my fingers around his girth.

At my tender touch, Kalun groaned and leaned back on the seat, relaxing and letting out his breath.

I began to move my hands ever-so-slowly and delicately up and down his shaft, just to see how he was going to react.

Kalun's eyes rolled back in his head. He looked like he was in ecstasy. His inner thighs began to lightly quiver. His thick cock was literally vibrating in my hands with arousal.

His breathing quickened as I slowly but surely increased the speed and length of my strokes.

I didn't think it possible, but his mammoth cock was growing even larger in my hands, as it engorged further with rushing blood and lust.

Clear, silky pre-cum began to ooze from the tip. I used it as a natural lubricant to glide my hands up and down his gloriously long, thick shaft. Kalun continued to groan with pleasure. He was almost in a trance, his eyes glazed with elation.

Emboldened by his reaction, I tightened my hands around his cock and thrust with more fervor.

"Does it feel good?" I whispered.

Kalun opened his eyes and stared at me with a hunger burning in his irises.

"In…incredible," he panted, barely able to speak through the waves of joy.

As I stroked him with increasing speed, his orc scent rose in potency, intoxicating my senses with primal lust.

I leaned forward and ran my tongue across one of his nipples.

He threw his head back and moaned with more intensity.

Encouraged, I began darting my tongue across his hard

nipple, flicking it and teasing it mercilessly, all the while pumping his hard shaft in my delicate hands.

"*Oh God*," he cried out to the Heavens.

I glanced down at his thick, veiny cock. I relished the fact that I was totally in control, feeding out the pleasure with the speed of my strokes. I was in full charge of this lust-filled, primal beast, and it thrilled me.

"Can I touch you?" Kalun asked, breathlessly. He was sweating and panting hard now.

He looked like he might be close to the finish line so I eased my motion. I wanted to prolong his pleasure.

My cheeks burned hot at his suggestion, but I nodded...both nervous and excited at the prospect of his hands exploring every curve and crevice I had.

Kalun's hands wandered over my pert breasts. He cupped them in his hands and squeezed them gently, grinning with joy at the touch. He leaned in and snaked his huge tongue across my nipples, flicking them before sucking and teasing them. They turned as hard as stone under his delicious onslaught. Ripples of pleasure radiated out from my chest.

He then trailed his tongue up my chest, along my neck, and around my chin before running it over my bottom lip and into my hungry mouth. Our tongues danced together feverishly.

I was completely enamored with him. A heat began to build in my center and spread throughout the rest of my body like wildfire.

Kalun stroked my tummy before slowly trailing his hand down and reaching the soaking slit between my legs. He locked eyes with me and smiled mischievously.

He seemed to relish the heat of the moment, teasing me before he would give me his touch. It was delicious torture, and I quivered with arousal as he searched my eyes intensely.

Finally, after what seemed like an eternity, he gently pushed the sensitive flesh between my legs apart. His fingers began to explore my intimate folds and creases.

I gasped as his large index finger made contact with my sensitive clit. He began to rub my engorged nub in a delicate circular motion, creating ripples of pleasure.

I briefly stopped jerking Kalun, immersed in the euphoria, before I remembered we were pleasuring each other.

"Sorry," I said, feeling myself blush. "I got distracted. It just feels *so*—"

I couldn't get the words out. I simply whimpered and moaned as Kalun slayed my clit with his expert hand, building the intensity and joy coursing through my body.

"It's okay, there are no rules to this," he assured, before increasing the speed and pressure of his heavenly touch on my electrified clit.

He grinned as he watched me squirm on top of him. I couldn't control my movement. My hips bucked involuntarily at his expert strokes.

"You like it?" Kalun asked, with an enamored expression.

"No," I whispered. "I love—"

I lost my words again as another involuntarily moan escaped from my throat.

"Do you want me to make you come?" Kalun asked, his face devilishly handsome to me, his jawline tight and defined, despite the stitches.

"Yes…" I murmured.

"Beg me for it, then," Kalun said, clearly enjoying himself now.

He seemed emboldened by my moans of ecstasy, which had

brought out his playful side.

"*Please*, make me come," I whined breathlessly, pleading with him for sweet release of the roiling energy that was building inside me.

"I'm not sure that will do," he said, teasing me further.

"Please master, allow your subservient slave to come, you own me," I added, joining in his little game.

The words must have excited him as more milky pre-cum oozed from the tip of his shaft. My hands were soaked and slippery as I continued stroking him until he once more groaned with contentment.

He leaned in and kissed me. My heart galloped and my breathing quickened.

Kalum placed a large finger at the entrance of my soaking pussy and gently explored my engorged lips. At the same time his thumb swirled in mind-altering circles around my clit, driving me crazy. I felt electrified. A puddle of wetness formed between my legs, my own lake of desire.

Kalun continued to caress my clit, sending me to the stars, then pushed his index finger inside me. I couldn't breathe — I was so overcome by the intimate sensation.

Fueled by my moans and increasing wetness, Kalun slipped another finger inside me with ease, probing my juicy hole.

"You feel so warm and wet," Kalun said, a hungry expression on his face and an erotic gleam in his eyes. "I can't get enough of your soaking pussy."

"It's yours, Kalun, all yours," I replied between gasping breaths. "Do whatever you want with me, my master."

Kalun maintained his intense gaze as he pushed his fingers further inside me, burying them to the knuckles.

He wiggled them around, exploring my hungry pussy,

caressing its internal surfaces. I gasped and quivered with delight as he began thrusting his fingers in and out of me, slow at first, then with more vigor…harder…faster…harder…faster…until I felt like the energy inside me was going to implode.

Not once did he break eye contact as he slipped his soaking fingers in and out of me at frenetic speed. He searched my face as I screamed with pleasure, his thumb sweetly assaulting my clit, heightening the sheer euphoria.

I arched my back and bucked my hips on Kalun's lap as he grazed my insides with his huge fingers, finding special spots on my back wall that sent pulses of pleasure radiating out every time he hit them.

I responded by thrusting my hands animatedly up and down his rock-hard shaft, hoping I could give him a fraction of the pleasure he was giving me.

His erotic, earthy orc scent once again flooded my senses, sending me into a sexual delirium. His fingers were practically a blur now, sliding effortlessly in and out of my greedy pussy. I couldn't hold back the orgasm for much longer. My climax was crawling its way through my body, and it would soon enrapture me, taking complete control.

"You're soaked," Kalun said, his eyes wide with surprise and delight.

I was slipping on his lap now, as I had released so much wetness at his thrilling touch.

Kalun's thick fingers probed my pussy even deeper, even faster.

"I don't think I can hold it anymore," I whined.

"Permission is required," he said, playfully.

"*Please* master, *please*, this slave *needs* to come. I *beg* your permission," I cried.

"No," he said flatly before darting his fingers inside me even deeper and harder, hitting my pleasure spots repeatedly, all the while flicking my sensitive clit with his thumb. He then leaned forwards and took my nipple in his month, rolling it with his lips before sucking on it hard.

I screamed at the top of my lungs "PLEASE!" as waves of pleasure cascaded through my body, joining together to form a tidal wave of ecstasy. I was in danger of literally exploding.

"Permission granted," said Kalun, then leaned in and kissed my neck. His fingers were still wedged deep inside me, making me feel wonderfully unhinged.

I arched my back, raised my head to the Heavens and screamed.

I was taken to another dimension as I came. It was so violent, so compelling, like a current ripping me apart. I surrendered to the ecstasy, an almost out-of-body experience that was enrapturing me and turning me to sweet mush.

Kalun didn't remove his fingers from inside my pussy, nor did he slow his motion. He kept wiggling them around, enhancing and prolonging the tidal wave of pure bliss. I bucked on top of him, convulsing and trembling as the sexual energy dissipated from my body.

Kalun studied me the entire time, never taking his eyes off my face in my most intimate of moments.

He must have been turned on by my display because he wasn't far behind me.

I roped my hands around his cock and began pumping, angling his tip so it was facing towards me. He groaned and writhed, his orc scent becoming even more heady and intoxicating.

I had no idea what compelled me to do it, but I placed the fingers of one hand deep inside my own pussy until they were soaked in my juices, then brought them up to his face. Wide-eyed, he opened his mouth hungrily and sucked my fingers, lapping up every drop of the wetness.

I wrapped both hands around his cock again and began pumping it furiously as I leaned forward and pushed my tongue into his mouth. Our tongues overlapped furiously and I could taste my own sweet pussy juices. It was a thrilling sensation.

Our sloppy tongue kiss was enough to send Kalun over the edge.

With a loud, primal groan he unloaded a volcanic spray of hot, white cum — splattering my body. It ran down my breasts and stomach, before soaking my inner thighs and pussy. It felt so warm and intimate to be showered by his seed.

Kalun gasped hard. He looked like he was in paradise. I didn't stop stroking his pulsing cock. The cum kept shooting out of his tip like molten lava. A spurt flew up and landed on my lower lip. I lapped at it with my tongue, tasting the sweet and salty fluid.

My body was drenched in his cum. It was sticky, warm and fantastic.

Only after I was sure that every last drop had been expelled onto my receptive body did I stop pumping his still-erect cock.

Once Kalun snapped out of his post-climax stupor and we had both composed ourselves somewhat, he gave me a sheepish grin. "I'm sorry…it's a lot to clean up."

"I don't mind at all," I said, giving him a mischievous smile. "The more the better, as far as I'm concerned."

Kalun breathed a sigh of relief, then paused to contemplate.

"You made me feel so good," he said, earnestly. "Not just the sex. You were…are…just what I need."

I stroked the side of his cheek where he sustained the injury.

"I want to be here for you, Kalun," I said. "Never forget, you are beautiful to me, and you always will be."

We kissed deeply and hugged each other tightly, not ever wanting to let go.

Finally, he gently lifted me from his lap.

I stood by the hearth while he grabbed a cloth to mop up the cum from my body. He gently caressed my body with the cloth using tender care.

I looked up. Through a small crack in the drapes I could see stars in the dark sky.

We both washed up in the bathroom before Kalun cooked a simple, yet delicious, meal of pheasant with a type of mashed parsnip I had never tried before.

Later, in bed, we held each other tight.

This evening was the most intimate experience I'd ever had in my life. I felt safe and sheltered wrapped in Kalun's huge arms.

My eyelids were heavy and I knew I would succumb to sleep very soon.

Swaddled in the warmth of Kalun's body, I nestled into the nook of his arm. He cradled me while I draped an arm across his wide chest to hold him firm to me.

I felt like we were two lost souls battered by the elements. We had found shelter and refuge together. For now, at least, we could ignore the storm battering the world outside and enjoy the warmth and comfort of each other's embrace.

Chapter Eight

I was the first to wake the next morning.

It was always in the first few moments of waking that I felt unburdened and serene. As always, I thanked the Creator for the new day and wished peace and prosperity to all living things.

I glanced to my right. The giant mound of Kalun was sleeping soundly beside me, his chest rising and falling like a living mountain. Every now and then, he would release a groan or a snort, followed by a long, drawn-out breath.

It was clear he was still deeply submerged in slumber.

I climbed as quietly as I could out of the bed, not wanting to disturb the sleeping giant of an orc.

My mind began replaying everything I'd done with him last night.

It had been an amazing, magical time that gave me a thrill just to think back on it.

I'd only brought myself to orgasm once or twice in my life, and that was long before I'd sworn my vows. The release I'd experienced with Kalun was bliss. I would even go so far to say that it lifted my soul.

A part of me still harbored guilty feelings due to my vows.

While the convent was a dark and dreadful place, the sisterly vows remained pure and timeless. They were the ideals that the convent should have embraced and advocated.

However, Kalun was pure of heart and spirit. Without having anything to do with human religion or the ways of the righteous path, he embodied the very principles that the sisterhood was striving to uphold. I could not berate myself for being attracted to him or comforting him in his time of need. A spark had been ignited between us and I was excited to see where it would lead.

I grabbed my tunic then slowly padded out of the bedroom into the living area, where I dressed. I drew back the drapes on the window to allow the light of dawn to spill into the cabin.

Seeing the slowly illuminating landscape, I was suddenly hit by a pang of guilt.

Nya had been expecting me to return last night. I hoped I hadn't worried her with my absence. However, she knew I'd be safe in the village and that I knew my way back to her cabin. I quickly surmised that she had worked out what had transpired between myself and Kalun; hence she didn't come looking for me. My cheeks blushed at the thought.

I fixed my gaze out of the window to distract my mind.

The sky was in its transition phase, the magical time when it's hard to distinguish between dawn and twilight. The heavens were painted a subtle silvery-lavender color. It was enough to awaken my soul. I bowed my head and once again gave thanks for the miracle of creation.

Movement outside captured my attention. I narrowed my

eyes, scrutinizing the view more intensely.

All the dwellings in the village were set in a perimeter around the main communal square. Kalun's cabin was perched on the outer edge, close to a small field that separated the village from the forest.

As more rays of light slowly began to bath the village, I could make out the activity.

It seemed the village was wasting no time in preparing for tomorrow's raid on the convent.

I saw orcs carrying large leather hides, no doubt to be cut and sewn into the customary battle dress. I saw others beginning to set up machinery outside. Two large orcs were carrying a metal contraption out of a shed and were heading towards the main square. It had a large wheel at the front and belts and pulleys, which appeared to operate the device. It dawned on me that it was a blade-sharpening instrument. Human villages had the equivalent devices, though this one was much larger.

Narag's orders — delivered through Vakar — must have quickly made their way through the village, judging by the speed of response.

But it was Kalun I thought of now. As captain of the guards, he should be orchestrating the preparations, not hidden away in his cabin. My heart sank at the thought.

"Good morning," a low voice rumbled behind me.

I jumped in surprise, a hand flying up to my chest to calm my suddenly thumping heart.

I spun around quickly, startled by Kalun's abrupt entrance.

He was dressed in his leather loin covering but was shirtless, his bulging biceps and boulder-like shoulders catching the light.

He had a sheepish smile on his face, as if he felt coy that I had woken up in his cabin.

"Good morning," I said, standing defensively with my back to the window, offering him a guarded smile.

He didn't seem annoyed that I had opened the drapes but, at the same time, he made no effort to step closer to the window.

I approached him, instead.

Kalun's face lit up as I closed the distance between us. His green eyes shimmered with warmth. He cupped my chin in his enormous hands and planted a kiss on the top of my forehead. I was relieved to feel his tender touch.

A tiny part of me had feared I would be unceremoniously booted from his cabin, now that his lust from yesterday had been satiated. However, as soon as he stood in front of me, I realized that the connection between us had not fizzled out after our intimate contact.

In fact, now that he was towering right in front of me, huge and ripped with muscles from head to toe, I was beginning to get worked up again, and a gentle tingle began stirring between my legs.

As I gazed deep into Kalun's eyes, I realized something that I hadn't been expecting. He was happy. He was cheerful and didn't look distraught or crippled by anxiety. My intervention must have helped in some way, I told myself.

"Thank you for being with me last night," Kalun said, by way of confirmation. "It was much better than being alone."

"I will stay here for as long as you need me," I assured him, reaching up to stroke his olive cheek.

His eyes twinkled with warmth. "I appreciate that. Would you care for some breakfast?"

I cast him a tenderhearted smile as my stomach began to rumble with hunger.

"Yes, please. That sounds great."

Kalun set to work in the kitchen as I continued monitoring the activity outside the window.

The ever-advancing sunrise allowed me to see more clearly now.

A group of needle-workers, both male and female, were clustered in a circle, diligently working on preparing new battle armor. Their nimble fingers stitched, threaded, buckled and clasped pieces of tough leather together. I saw that these completed pieces were then taken to another area where the fearsome tusks and spikes were attached.

Youngsters were using rags to shine leather and bone tusks at a table. They joked and laughed as they worked, no doubt feeling proud to be involved in the battle preparations.

The machine that I had seen being carried earlier was now in operation. The large wheel revolved at speed while a burly orc repeatedly pressed down on a pedal, which operated the pulley mechanism. Another orc, older and shorter in stature, pressed the blades of knives and swords against the spinning wheel, sending sparks flying. The shorter orc, who I took to be the master craftsman, would hold the blades up to the light, examining the serrated edges carefully before once again running them against the spinning circular stone.

A little further down, yet more orcs were hooking chains onto heavy stone balls, which were embedded with intimidating spikes. These were the weapon of choice for the orcs, and I had personally seen them used to devastating effect against the atrocious ogre Grimkerag-Triegrut.

My eyes roamed to the far perimeter of the village.

There, out in the field, the warriors were taking part in training drills and exercises. Clad in their brown leather battle armor, faces stoic and set, they moved as one entity across the field like a wall of unyielding strength. Each individual member of the guard was tall and muscled, but it was when they moved together in tight formation that they took on a truly intimidating presence.

I realized that Kalun should be out there leading their efforts; he just needed to break through his fear. It was ironic that the orc captain had no hesitation in putting his life on the line in combat, yet when it came to a potential loss of honor, fear appeared to cripple him. It certainly seemed odd to me, but I reminded myself that I was in no position to pass judgment on a culture that I had very little knowledge about.

A few minutes later, Kalun brought me fresh scrambled eggs and a slice of toasted bread. I salivated as I watched a melting slab of butter sliver across its surface, leaving a golden streak in its wake.

I took the plate and sat on a seat close to the hearth.

"Wow," I grinned, looking at the food. "This looks amazing. Not only are you a warrior, but you can also cook."

It was by no means a subtle reminder of his position, but it was the best I could come up in the moment.

"I manage," Kalun said, with a thoughtful expression.

He looked up and gave me a humble smile. I could tell that he didn't like the spotlight. He was too modest, which was an endearing trait, but I wished he would give himself more credit. There was no reason he should lack confidence in himself.

I glanced outside the window and saw that the warriors were jogging in our direction as part of their drills. I didn't waste the opportunity.

I pointed outside the window. "Do you recognize those guards?"

I asked the question in the most innocent tone I could muster.

Even so, Kalun began to behave evasively. He made a grunt of acknowledgement, but otherwise said nothing. He turned his back away from the scene unfolding outside and began walking towards the kitchen. I sighed.

"Kalun?" I called out behind him.

"Yes?" He tossed a wary glance at me over his shoulder.

"Is everything alright?" I asked.

"Yes, it is fine," he said, not very convincingly.

"If there is something you want to talk—"

He spun around, cutting in sharply. "I do not." His features immediately softened. "I am...sorry. It is just..."

He didn't seem able to find the right words to express himself.

I decided to take a more direct approach. I placed my plate on the seat and approached him.

"You are captain of the guards, Kalun," I said, not unkindly. "Shouldn't you be out there leading the preparations?"

I knew I had overstepped an invisible boundary, but I had to tackle the issue head on. I also recalled that yesterday it was only a bold — you might say impolite — move on my part that made him finally reveal his face.

"I...cannot." Kalun's shoulders sagged and anxiety dulled his usually bright eyes. "I would frighten the young ones." His voice was laced with melancholy.

"The way you look hasn't changed who you are," I encouraged. "I have already looked past the wound; others will do the same."

"I doubt it," he replied. "My men will lose respect for me. It is...was...my role to be an inspiration, a guide...someone for them to look up to. That cannot be the case now with this appearance. Why would the troops want to go into battle with me — a captain of the guards who could not defend himself against an ogre? They will rightly worry that I cannot protect them, if I can't even protect myself."

I hadn't even thought about his injury from that perspective.

"You are making an assumption," I quickly countered. "You cannot know how others will react. Also, please take a moment to think about it. You have a battle scar because you were in a *battle* — with a murderous ogre twice your size. You came out on top and rescued me. I can only see honor in that accomplishment."

I gently rested my hand on his forearm.

Kalun lifted his gaze, but gave me a disheartened look.

"None of them will take me seriously. My face looks like a battered piece of meat."

He hung his head in shame.

I squeezed his arm consolingly.

"They will see what I see — someone who is strong, brave, loyal and noble."

I was doing my best to encourage him but, based on his downcast expression, it didn't seem my efforts were paying off. He refused to look at me. His eyes were rooted to the floor.

"I am...ashamed." Kalun winced, as if it pained him to say the words aloud.

He was vulnerable, wearing his heart on his sleeve.

"What are you ashamed of?" I whispered soothingly.

Kalun blinked, but he still wouldn't look at me.

"I do not want my gruesome face to distract the warriors. I do not want mothers and their young to fear me or cower in my presence when I come near them. This is a distraction that the village does not need, especially at this critical juncture."

"I promise you, it won't be like that," I reassured him, continuing to stroke his arm. "Your wound will serve as a reminder of who you are. The orcs will feel safe in your presence, because you are willing to put your own life on the line to shield others from harm."

He looked doubtful. This approach clearly wasn't working.

With a heavy heart, I decided to try one last strategy. If I had overstepped a boundary before, I was now about to leapfrog over it. But I felt it was time to throw caution to the wind.

"You know, better than anyone, what it is like to face an ogre — the damage those beasts can inflict," I said, rather too harshly. "Tomorrow, your troops, the orcs you have trained and served alongside, may have to face a countless number of them."

Kalun looked up, concern flaring in his eyes.

However, I would not relent.

"I don't know how many warriors will come back to the village at the end of the day tomorrow. But one thing that I *do* know with certainty is that each and every one of them stands a better chance of survival if you are training them and guiding them today, and if you are leading them tomorrow. They *need* you Kalun, now more than ever."

His eyes were wide with shock, and with sudden realization, it seemed. My words had landed like physical blows on him.

He looked out of the window at the warriors — his warriors — then took a deep breath before straightening his posture and tightening his strong jawline.

He took my hand and cupped it, giving it an affectionate squeeze.

"I do not deserve you," he said, simply.

I sincerely hoped that meant I had reawakened the warrior within him.

"Will you accompany me?" he asked, in a hopeful tone.

I nodded vigorously, relief flooding me. "It would be my absolute honor."

We gobbled up our breakfasts and Kalun dressed in his battle armor.

He was a sight to behold standing in front of me, stately and gallant, every inch a fearless leader.

He wore his helmet, with imposing cream-colored tusks protruding from the sides, as well as armor plates on his shoulders, and around his waist and wrists.

I scanned him breathlessly — hopelessly attracted not only to his brooding physical presence, but also the nobility of his character.

As we approached the front door, I noticed that Kalun was a little hesitant.

"What's wrong?" I asked.

He took a deep breath to prepare himself. "I just need a moment."

"One step at a time," I advised. "I'll be right there alongside you."

Kalun glanced down at me, a subtle gleam of encouragement lit up his bright green eyes.

"You are right," he acknowledged, giving me a nod. "One step at a time, but I just need to get it over with."

I grinned at him. "That's the spirit."

He opened the door to the outside world.

I didn't take for granted how big of a step this was for him.

We slowly wandered away from the cabin together and

approached the central square.

As we neared the throng of activity, warriors and villagers alike stopped what they were doing and simply stared at him.

I winced internally. This is exactly what I *didn't* want to happen.

The troops halted mid-step, while the crafters downed their tools.

I couldn't breathe. How could I have been so wrong? This was a huge mistake.

Then, one by one, each orc raised their right hand to their chest and balled it into a fist. They began rhythmically banging the area right over the hearts, at the same time bowing very slightly.

I knew exactly what they were doing. They were putting on a show of solidarity and support for Kalun, restoring to him the honor and respect that he both deserved and needed right now.

Kalun made the same thumping gesture with his right hand before bowing slightly and then resuming his march forwards.

There was a renewed purpose in his step as he squared his shoulders and lifted his head a little higher. His demeanor had shifted from defensive to far more assertive.

I noticed as we walked that the passing soldiers would pay him their respects.

"*Dinshaluk-Mohrical,*" they would call out.

"*Dinshaluk-Ephareem,*" Kalun would reply, solemnly.

Kalun approached a row of guards who were similar in size and stature to him. They were dressed in the same warrior attire, but the horns on their helmets were noticeably smaller. They stood upright to salute him with curious gazes. They were obviously studying his wound, but Kalun didn't appear disturbed.

"Captain…are you…well?" a tall and stocky warrior asked, taking a step closer to peer at Kalun with inquisitiveness. His features were marked with concern.

My muscles seized with trepidation, but Kalun maintained his composure. He didn't seem to flinch at the close attention.

"I am faring well," Kalun declared. I noticed his body stiffening a little, but otherwise he was in complete control.

"Are you recovering?" another of the warriors asked, smaller in stature than the first, but equally as worried as he peered at the scar on Kalun's face, without explicitly mentioning it.

"I assure you, I am healing nicely," Kalun advised with an insistent nod, drawing in a deep breath. "However, your concern for my welfare is duly noted and appreciated."

Whispers of relief began to circulate amongst the troops.

I smiled as I saw how much affection they had for their captain, and how genuinely concerned they were for his well-being.

"We heard about you taking out the ogre," another guard declared, more boldly.

"Yes," Kalun confirmed. "I took him down with the brave assistance of Vakar."

"Vakar said he was the biggest bastard he'd ever seen," the guard replied. "You need to show us how, Captain — we all want to take one down tomorrow."

Cheers rang out among the soldiers.

"Rest assured," said Vakar. "After my inspection rounds, I will be right back here to show you how."

"And tomorrow, Captain?" said the same orc, expectantly. "You will be leading us on the raid?"

Kalun nodded. "Where else would I be?"

More cheers rang out amongst his troops.

I felt my heart swell as we moved on.

As we weaved through the villagers working in the central square, Kalun would stop every few feet to shake hands or give words of advice. Sometimes he would simply offer a brief word of motivation or praise, which seemed to raise morale. The orcs couldn't help noticing Kalun's wound, but it didn't seem to faze him all that much anymore.

Little by little, I noticed Kalun's confidence blossoming. He was walking and talking with purpose and resolve, engaged in the battle preparations with no thought to his own condition.

His final stop was at the sharpening station, where the master weaponsmith was still honing blades. Kalun inspected the weapons and offered high praise for the skill and precision used to get the weapons into pristine condition.

After a few more minutes in the square, we broke away from the crowd.

"I need to visit the prison area to check on Morgut," Kalun advised me, with a cautious expression. "It is part of my duties."

I remembered that Morgut was the former village chief who had been overthrown after he had attempted to murder baby Armaan. A shudder ran down my spine.

"I can go with you," I said, not relishing the prospect, but keen to maintain my support for Kalun. Besides, seeing the workings of the village was enlightening for me.

Kalun gave me an apprehensive glance, but finally relented.

The holding area was on the outskirts of the village at the opposite side from where we were. We had a long walk ahead of us.

As we made off, we once again passed the warriors doing their battle drills. Salutes were exchanged and Kalun assured them he would be back soon to take charge of the training.

Several minutes later we arrived at an imposing cabin, which looked like it had been reinforced with many layers of strong wood. It looked big enough to house several cells inside.

There were two enormous guards standing at the entrance with aggressive scowls on their faces. But as soon as they noticed Kalun approaching, they gave him a respectful salute. The guards gave dutiful nods of approval as we passed into the jail without having to offer an explanation of why we were there.

Unlike the residential cabins, the prison had dirt floors. The inside was cold, dim and had a musty smell.

An unsettled feeling sank deep into my bones. It was difficult for me to return to a prison environment, even if I wasn't the one in captivity. It stirred unpleasant memories of being caged in the convent basement by Vitora and her sadistic Senior Sisters.

I wrapped my arms around my chest protectively and walked closer to Kalun. He roped an enormous arm around my waist and escorted me along, a wordless gesture that gave me an assurance that he wouldn't let anything happen to me.

Morgut's jail cell was at the very end of the narrow hallway. I peered in.

The conditions were basic. There was only a cot for him to lay on with a thin, threadbare blanket on top. Having experienced life as a prisoner, I almost felt sorry for him. That was until he opened his hateful mouth.

"Look who it is — the back-stabbing traitor," Morgut said, his lips twisting into a snarky smile. "With a human whore no less," he added, cutting me a look of loathing.

I noticed Kalun stiffening beside me.

Morgut was small in stature and the by far the oldest orc I had seen so far. His face was lined with age and his eyes were small and cruel, almost rodent-like.

He had been sitting at the far end of the cell with his back to the wall. But he now stood to his full, rather insubstantial, height. I noticed a prominent tattoo on this chest of a sun and moon intertwined — no doubt a tribal symbol of his former authority.

"What happened to your face, traitor?" Morgut chided, then cackled with laughter, pointing at Kalun and metaphorically rubbing salt into a wound. "You were ugly before, but now you are truly hideous."

Kalun didn't rise to the bait.

Morgut moved closer to the wooden jail bars and coiled his gnarly fingers around them. Dirt was caked under his fingernails. He was far shorter than Kalun, about my height in fact, and had a messy tuft of graying hair on his head. He wore a scornful scowl.

"Did your bitch do that to you during sex?" Morgut chastised, laughing wickedly again, as he nudged his chin in my direction. "Likes it rough, does she? Just leave her with me, I'll show her what rough really is."

Kalun flinched and took a step forward, brooding over Morgut, even through the jail bars.

"Keep a civil tongue in your head and have some respect," Kalun warned.

"She's a filthy human bitch," Morgut said, shrugging indifferently. "She deserves no respect. She is part of the disease that has infected our race."

Kalun balled his fists, fuming.

I placed a placating hand on his shoulder.

He let out a deep breath and then straightened his fingers again.

"I think you are hardly in a position to call someone else filthy," Kalun said, calmly.

"Maybe you should take a look at yourself, captain," Morgut spat back. "I may be filthy, but you are *repugnant* —a monster." He once again let out a thunderous cackle. "You expect to lead the warriors with a face like *that*?"

Now it was my turn to ball my fists. At this point I was mentally urging Kalun to punch him into the back wall.

Morgut was judging the other orcs by his own low, hateful standards. I dearly wished he could have seen how the warriors had in fact treated Kalun.

"You are no longer in charge, Morgut. Your words are mere wind," stated Kalun, maintaining his composure. "You may think you still hold power but, if you had not noticed, you are rotting inside a cell."

"You have *no idea* what kind of power I hold," Morgut spat back.

His words — the conviction with which he uttered them — took me aback.

"If you think for one second that I won't have my revenge, you are sorely mistaken, old friend," he added.

Kalun simply glared at him. "You are no friend of mine."

He took my arm and we hastily departed down the hallway.

All the while Morgut was shouting vows to seek revenge. They seemed like empty threats to me, but were disturbing to hear, nonetheless. I was left with an unsettled feeling in the pit of my stomach.

As soon as I exited the prison, an invisible weight lifted off my chest and I could finally breathe again.

I thanked the Heavens that I had never stepped foot in this village while Morgut was in charge. I also expressed gratitude that the fate of the orcs was now in the wise and protective hands of Narag and his noble commanding warriors, including Vakar and Kalun.

"Sorry you had to hear that," said Kalun, turning to me.

"It was my choice to come," I reminded him. "I'm sure his bark is a lot worse than his bite."

"Let us hope so," he replied, seemingly a little disturbed by the encounter also.

We headed back towards the central square.

Once there, we briefly hugged before we went our separate ways.

Kalun took command of the training drills while I headed off towards Nya's cabin. I felt I owed her a personal apology after my disappearing act the previous evening. Plus, I couldn't wait to tell her about me and Kalun.

Chapter Nine

It was dusk and I was sitting with Kalun on the porch of his cabin. There was a reflective silence between us, but it was comfortable and soothing.

The frenetic activity of the day was winding down in the village, and soon it would be the calm before the storm.

We were perfectly content to sit there watching the sunset beyond the horizon. The sky had a warm amber glow as the orange fireball of the sun disappeared behind the tree line of the dense forest just beyond the village.

Crickets trilled in the distance. Insects buzzed in the trees and shrubs nearby.

Even on the cusp of battle, the external environment was surprisingly serene. But it was difficult to block out the anxieties swimming around my head: Kalun heading off to battle tomorrow, the brutal ogres, and the long-suffering convent sisters. There were so many factors and unknowns.

Kalun's gentle voice interrupted my spiraling thoughts.

"I just wanted to thank you again," he said, turning his head to give me a tender smile.

"For what?"

"The way you encouraged me to face my fears today. Without you, I probably would have remained locked away in my cabin feeling sorry for myself. You gave me strength when I needed it."

I placed a hand on his forearm. "That strength *always* resided within you, Kalun."

He gently brushed his hand on top of mine.

"No one else bothered to check on me after the wound was stitched," he continued, gazing at the horizon. "It is not that they did not care, but we orcs tend to only take account of physical injuries. As you rightly told me, sometimes the deepest wound cannot be seen."

I admired him for stepping out of his comfort zone today. He no longer had to worry about being judged by his fellow villagers, or his warriors. No one thought differently of him just because he had a prominent scar across his face. Kalun felt he had earned back his respect which, in truth, he had never lost in the first place.

He lightly stroked my arm, filling me with a tingling warmth. Every time we touched, even if it was in the briefest, most innocent of ways, it sent a rejuvenating current rippling through my body that left me craving more.

Kalun inhaled then slowly turned to face me. I saw compassion and affection flickering in his bright eyes.

"I just want you to know that I…appreciate…you," he said, rather coyly.

"Well, I…appreciate…you, too," I replied, with the tiniest of smirks. "Especially as I'm alive to witness this beautiful sunset thanks to you."

His face took on a more serious expression. I could see him contemplating, trying to find his next words.

"That does not mean you owe me anything, Hana," he said, solemnly. "Nor did you ever owe me anything."

I reached out for his giant hand and intertwined our fingers.

"It was never my intention to come to your cabin to try to… even the balance…because you saved my life," I said. "I gave of myself with my own free will, mind and heart, which is where you will always dwell for me."

I gripped his fingers more tightly. His eyes appeared a little wet.

"Also, I see incredible potential in you, Kalun. You have natural gifts, and it would be a tragedy to watch them go to waste. The world needs you to make it a better, kinder place."

Kalun's features warmed.

"It's funny…" he trailed off.

"What is?" I quizzed, gazing up at him.

"I am this honored warrior, captain of the guards, and have been for many years. I have been on the front lines of many horrendous battles. I have had to fight off atrocious beasts that would put that lumbering ogre to shame. The irony is not lost on me that, as a warrior, I needed your patient help to simply walk out of the front door. The judgement of my peers held more fear for me than any army of ferocious enemies. It hardly makes sense — even to me."

"We can *all* be guilty of failing to confront our fears, and it is to our detriment," I said. "The one good thing about being in the convent, apart from my sisters, was that it encouraged the nurturing of the spirit as well as the body. Those things that we refuse to confront grow stronger in the shadows, until they control us. It is the light of day that chases away the darkness."

"Wise words," Kalun replied.

He took my hand and looked deep into my eyes, then slowly and methodically kissed each knuckle of my fingers.

"I usually keep my emotional barricades up," he confided. "In fact, until you came along, those walls were impenetrable."

He paused for a moment before continuing, weighing his words.

"But with you…it is so…*different.* The connection and freedom I feel with you — it is something that I cannot explain. The purity of your heart is translucent."

"Well," I began with a humble chuckle, placing a hand to my heart. "I am *hardly* without imperfections, but I appreciate the sweet compliment."

His eyes were cast in contemplative shadow.

"It has been a long time since I have been able to enjoy companionship like this," he said.

I understood exactly where he was coming from.

"Me too," I agreed. "I hadn't realized how truly lonely I was until I came here. The convent basement and dreadful ogre caves almost broke me. I can't describe how exquisite it is to be here, surrounded by those who have your wellbeing at heart. Even though we are on the eve of…of…."

I swallowed hard, tripping on my words. I didn't want to contemplate tomorrow. I couldn't bear the thought of Kalun never coming back to me, when I had only just found him.

He gently squeezed my hand again. "You do not have to be alone anymore, Hana, in spirit or in body."

He gave me a smoldering look of yearning. I knew what he was thinking without him having to utter a single word. In this magical setting — as the low sun painted the sky in deep russet hues — I felt like I could tap the secrets of his soul. The longing shimmering reflectively in his eyes was unmistakable.

I was the first one to break our sensuous gaze. It was so fierce, it took my breath away and made me tremble with anticipation.

The sun had almost completely set. Soon the sky's dark oranges would give way to the grayish hues of dusk, before quickly fading to an inky black, star-speckled night.

"It's getting late…" I trailed off, my cheeks burning slightly. "You will need to get a good night's rest. You need your energy for tomorrow."

Kalun's eyes glimmered. He leaned in close to me, making my heart drum excitedly. He smelled earthy and intoxicating. I was falling hard for him. I could no longer deny that fact.

"Sleep is *not* how I get fired up for battle," he said with a seductive smirk.

I returned his inviting look. "Is that so?"

Kalun got to his feet and stood in front of me, gazing down with a fondness that touched my heart. He guided his hand to my cheek and let his fingers slip across my jawline, gently soothing me with tender strokes.

He lightly brushed his fingers down my neck then up and down my shoulder and arm, sending a quiver of warmth pulsing through my body.

I gave him an enticing grin to wordlessly let him know I was more than receptive to his touch. I was drawn to him and keen to explore what this night had in store for us.

I also felt Kalun had the right idea. Physical touch was a natural soother, stabilizing the mind and balancing the spirit — easing stress and worries. Experiencing intimacy with Kalun also sounded like a fantastic way to wear myself out. Perhaps the *only* way either of us would find sleep tonight, with the heavy burden of tomorrow bearing down on us.

Kalun traced his fingers back up to my collarbone, still eyeing me with that intense look of yearning.

"You are exquisite in every way," he whispered, giving me a hungry look.

His massive body was now a silhouette. The sun had gone down and left us basking only in the aura of each other's presence.

"Thank you," I said in a whisper. His tender touch left me craving more.

I stood up and took a step closer to him. We were standing less than an inch apart, our bodies nearly touching.

"Whatever the new day brings, I am now complete in my soul for having known you," he said.

"Ssshh," I whispered. "Don't talk that way." I suddenly felt overcome.

He cupped his hands over my shoulders. "I will fight with every nerve and sinew in my body to return to you."

"That is a promise I intend to hold you to," I said.

He tenderly tucked loose strands of hair behind my ear, then leaned down and grazed his soft lips across my cheek. His mouth met with mine, and I felt one with the stars above.

Adrenaline pumped through my veins. I kissed him back hard as a current of emotions swept me off my feet — fear, longing, admiration, foreboding, anticipation and love — all mixing together to charge my body and spirit.

Kalun's breath quickened on my cheek and neck as he leaned down to shower my sensitive skin with voluptuous kisses.

"You and you alone, my *Eshtar*," he whispered, snaking his burly arms around my back and hugging me close to his rugged, expansive chest.

I placed my ear to his beating heart, roping my arms around his thick torso. It felt incredibly good to be held by Kalun, to be warm, safe and adored.

"You and you alone, my one true love," I said, echoing what I was almost certain he had said to me in the orc dialect.

Kalun cradled me close to his burly frame, stroking my hair adoringly.

I never wanted to let him go; I couldn't get enough of his tender touch. I was addicted to him, fueled by the way he nurtured me — the way we nurtured each other.

Wordlessly, Kalun lifted me in his powerful arms and slowly carried me inside to the bedroom. He placed me gently on the edge of the bed. My heart pounded with anticipation.

I gazed up at him, feeling intense, fevered longing ensnaring my senses. His iridescent olive eyes twinkled with raw, primal desire.

"I want you *so* badly," I said, absorbed in his intense gaze.

Kalun slipped my tunic up and over my body and gently laid me down on the bed. He opened my legs wide with his hands. My body began to tingle with anticipation. Kalun's eyes were wild with hunger. He licked his lips, practically salivating.

"Since your delicious wet fingers entered my mouth, I've been craving the taste of you again," he confided, gazing at me as if he were asking permission to feed on me.

"Do it, Kalun," I whispered in a breathless voice. "Devour me."

"With pleasure," he replied. A huge grin stretched across his face.

My legs quivered with excitement. I was dazed, fixated on Kalun.

He stroked my inner thighs with his fingertips. He was so

slow and delicate, ramping up my anticipation.

His fingertips barely grazed my skin. The movement was so tender and slight, but the sensation was electric, nevertheless. My skin raised with goose bumps. I was completely fascinated by the level of pleasure he could deliver with such subtle touches.

By the time he undressed and dropped to his knees in front of me, I was desperate for him.

Blood rushed to my clit and made it tingle with longing.

My legs trembled as Kalun traced his hands up my thighs then cupped them underneath my bottom, before leaning in close to my body.

He started peppering my inner thighs with delicate, lingering kisses, working his way higher and higher.

I was panting hard by the time he reached my moist pussy.

He gave me a frisky smile before burying his head between my legs.

He kissed my engorged lips and then gently pushed his tongue between my soft, warm and wet folds. He began to slowly lick and kiss every surface and crease of my vagina.

I was dripping with excitement at his sensual touch. My clit was swollen and pulsing excitedly. I arched my back and whimpered as Kalun slid his tongue across my erect nub. He kissed it, licked, sucked it, teased it.

His fragrant, earthy scent began to release from the pores of his skin as he worked my sensitive clit in a circular motion with his tongue, driving me wild. Every now and then, he would take it full in his mouth and gently suck, ramping up the euphoria.

His scent was subtle at first but, as he worked my clit with his strong tongue, it grew more potent — as did my desire. I was captivated by the aroma as it flooded my nostrils, filling me with passion and insatiable yearning.

Sensing my heighted lust, Kalun went in for the kill.

He inserted his long, powerful tongue in between my lips and then pushed it deep inside my hungry pussy.

I gasped at the intimate sensation. I felt unbelievably connected to him.

He pushed further in and wiggled his strong, eel-like tongue, exploring every corner and crevice of my wet hole.

I heard a gentle sucking sound as he drank down the juices flowing freely from my pussy, before darting his tongue back deep inside me. He hit a pleasure spot on my back wall that sent currents of ecstasy rippling through my quivering legs.

I gasped for breath as his powerful mating scent drove me into a sexual frenzy.

His tongue was working furiously inside me.

He devoured me. He destroyed me. He showed me no mercy.

I was bucking and shaking on the bed, but he did not relent. Instead he increased the ferocity of his tongue's probing while raising his hands to my chest and caressing my rock-hard nipples. He flicked and squeezed them while ramming his massive tongue deeper and deeper into my insatiable pussy.

I cuffed the sheets in my fists and screamed with euphoria. I was spinning out of control. A tidal wave of primal pleasure surged through me. I was soaring to paradise.

Kalun buried his face deeper between my legs as I squeezed my inner thighs against the sides of his head. I dug my heels into his back. He pressed his face even closer to my pussy and rammed his tongue in and out with ferocious speed, while pinching my nipples with more force.

"Kalun…" I trailed off, breathless and panting hard, lost in the throes of joy. It was an absolutely surreal moment for me. I had no idea the human body could receive this amount of pleasure.

He moved his hands down to my legs and began stroking them as he ate me out with a frenzied passion. I could tell he was urged on by my sensual moaning.

I was soaking with arousal. Passion pounded in my heart and fueled my body. He could go down on me for days like this and I wouldn't complain. I didn't need food or rest; his massive tongue wedged deep inside my moist pussy would sustain my body and soul. I was experiencing life-altering pleasure.

A current was spreading through my body. I was skirting near the edge. I didn't think I could hold back the orgasm much longer. Kalun's face was buried deep between my legs.

He coiled his hands around my bottom and raised me slightly, finding a better angle for his tongue to explore the furthest recesses of my hungry pussy. The level of intimacy was unreal.

I loved the way he feasted on me. He had an insatiable hunger. All the layers of inhibition I had were stripped away. There was nothing left but raw, intimate, glorious passion.

I opened my legs wider, granting him all the access he needed to slay my hole with his expert tongue.

His mouth moved up to my clit and he swirled it around in tight circles, sending me to the stars, before stabbing his giant tongue back inside my pussy deeper than it had ever been. The raised angle allowed him to hit every pleasure spot on my back wall. At the same time, he reached up and urgently flicked my erect nipples with his fingers.

I was utterly destroyed, and hurtled over the edge to a monumental climax. I arched my back, bucked my hips on his face and convulsed violently as euphoria flooded my body and soul.

Kalun obliterated me. A tidal wave of ecstasy rippled through me until I couldn't see straight. I forgot who I was, where I was. I only knew immeasurable joy.

As the thunderous orgasm enraptured my body, Kalun didn't relent from probing my pussy with his tongue, lapping against every crevice, leaving no part unexplored. His fingers caressed my nipples in a circular motion, sending currents of pleasure rippling across my chest.

I lost control. Involuntarily, I jerked my hips upwards and squirted a warm jet of cum from my convulsing pussy.

Kalun didn't miss a beat.

He opened his mouth wide to catch the gushing stream of liquid, a wide-eyed look of sheer delight on his face. He drank it down greedily before licking his lips, then used his tongue to lap up the remaining fluid dribbling down my thighs. He hunted down every drop, as if it was the sweetest nectar in the world. He ran his tongue over my pussy lips and clit to ensure nothing was missed.

I relaxed back on the bed, spent. My cheeks burned. My hair was a mess. I was sweaty and sticky. The sheets under my bottom were completely soaked.

Kalun came to my side and leaned in to gently kiss my forehead. But I was still so turned on by him that I grabbed his head and guided his mouth to mine instead.

I darted my tongue into his mouth and mashed it with his, tasting my own warm and sweet pussy juices. I was in heaven.

When we finally broke our extended lip-lock, Kalun held me close.

"You look so sexy when you come," he said, adoringly

stroking my hair. "It makes me so hard."

"Good," I said, staring into his eyes seductively. "Now I can return the favor."

My shuddering orgasm had fatigued me, but it wasn't going to stop me from giving Kalun an experience to remember.

"Only if you are comfortable with it," Kalun said, considerately.

I glanced down at his massive cock — swollen, erect and pointing proudly up at the ceiling.

My clit began to throb. I couldn't believe I was getting so worked up again, mere minutes after I'd had the most intense orgasm of my life.

But just looking at Kalun's delicious cock, engorged and pulsing, massively turned me on.

"There is *nothing* I want to do more," I said, breathlessly.

Kalun sat naked on the edge of the bed.

I got down on my knees in front of him.

I eyed him seductively as I coiled my hands around the bottom of his swollen shaft. He was *so* thick and *so* hard.

The tip of his cock was already dribbling silky, translucent pre-cum.

I playfully danced the top of my tongue across his tip, mopping up the sweet and salty fluid. It was warm, earthy and delicious.

His thighs quivered ever so slightly. A wild gleam filmed over his eyes. He began releasing his heavenly mating scent, which heightened my desire for him.

I was wildly excited, but also a little daunted by the sheer size of his cock.

"I might not be able to fit all of you in my mouth…" I trailed off sheepishly, but was still determined to impress him.

"I am going to love it no matter what," Kalun encouraged. "Because I am with you."

He reached out to affectionately stroke my cheek.

He was so good to me, so patient, so accepting and giving. What I wouldn't do for him.

With my hands still cuffed around the bottom of his shaft, I slowly lowered my mouth onto his cock, showering his swollen tip with soft kisses and gently licking its smooth, warm surface.

I could feel his entire shaft pulsing and throbbing in my hands with excitement.

I slid my tongue up and down his tip, grazing it gently on the underside. I cocked my head to the side and made smoldering eye contact with him as I greedily licked his pulsating flesh.

Kalun stiffened and moaned with pleasure; that was my cue to raise the stakes.

I wrapped my plump, soft lips over the tip of his cock, making a tight seal, and began to feed it ever-so-slowly into my mouth. When I had the entire head in my mouth, Kalun gave out a low, guttural moan of joy.

But I didn't stop with just the head. I kept going, feeding his shaft down my throat, taking as much of his length that I could. I was at least halfway down his shaft.

Kalun let out a primal roar and threw his head back in ecstasy.

His orc scent floored me with its extraordinary potency, fueling my lust — and my ambition.

I pushed down even harder, taking more of his mammoth cock into me. I couldn't believe how much of him I had managed to swallow down. It was a thrilling sensation.

Adrenaline pumped through my veins as I began slowly thrusting my head up and down on his cock, finding a rhythm.

His long shaft was wedged deep in my mouth and throat.

I took as much of him as I could without choking or gagging. I sheathed my lips tight around his girth and sucked hard while bobbing up and down.

Judging by his uncontrolled groans, Kalun was loving it.

He let out another spurt of silky pre-cum in response, but I didn't release his glorious cock from my hungry mouth. Instead, I allowed the warm, salty fluid to run down my throat and settle happily in my stomach. I wanted to guzzle down everything he had to offer.

Lost in heat and ecstasy, Kalun gently linked his hands around my head, guiding me as I pumped my mouth up and down on his shaft. He was controlling the speed and depth of my mouth, and I willingly submitted to this powerful, primal beast. It was a thrilling feeling to surrender myself like this.

Kalun's eager groans of pleasure became louder, more intense.

He began grinding his hips upwards in the same rhythm as his powerful hands were coaxing my head downwards, so my delicate mouth was speared over and over again by his rock-hard cock. Faster and deeper, faster and deeper he impaled me as his groans became more urgent.

I was massively turned on by my complete submission to him — my mouth and throat servicing his desire without any complaint or resistance from me. The sensation soaked my pussy with arousal. I could sense a lake of wetness between my legs as I became a willing plaything for his animalistic lust.

His giant cock was practically a blur now as it rammed me at ferocious speed. He released another spurt of pre-cum, which I swallowed down greedily. I was drunk on his orc scent and the sheer wild intensity of the moment.

He groaned and stiffened — I could sense he was close to the edge.

He took his hands away from my head, giving me the option to pull away as he prepared to shoot his load.

But I didn't back down. Fueled by my carnal lust, I did the exact opposite. I pushed my head down hard, swallowing even more of his delicious shaft.

He gasped, then his whole body stiffened. I could feel his cock quivering deep in my throat, then it suddenly became incredibly stiff.

In the next moment a tidal wave of cum released from his cock and shot down my throat. I greedily drank as much of it down as I could. It gushed down my throat, sticky, juicy, warm and salty. I kept my head wrapped around his cock for as long as I could, guzzling down his warm seed.

At the point where I felt I might gag, I released his pulsing cock from my mouth, sliding its length out quickly.

Cum was still erupting from his tip and I placed my tongue into the flow, lapping up the creamy fluid. His fountain of cum spilled over the sides of his tip and ran down his lengthy shaft.

I licked the entirety of his shaft up and down, hunting down the cum. I relished the way it made Kalun moan and quiver with delight.

I once more sucked on the tip of his cock, collecting the last spurts that were being released, then danced my tongue over his slit to ensure I had coaxed out every last drop of the delicious fluid.

My mouth, lips and chin were coated in his cum. I looked Kalun deep in the eyes before using my finger to collect the gooey liquid. I then placed it in my mouth, a look of dreamy delight on my face as I swallowed the still-warm creamy cum.

I then stood, leaned in and kissed him deeply. Our tongues danced together feverishly, mixing saliva, cum and my pussy juices into a heady cocktail that we both savored.

My performance must have taken Kalun aback. His eyes were wide as he collapsed back on the mattress, panting hard, caked with sweat. He stared at the ceiling, looking like he was in a trance.

I lay next to him and hooked my arms around his broad chest, hugging him tightly. We were still both breathing hard, coming down from the euphoria.

Once Kalun had finally calmed down enough to speak, he gave me an infatuated glance and a drowsy smile.

"This day has been full of surprises," he said playfully, stroking my hair as we lay together naked, sticky and exhausted.

I smiled, relishing the warmth and intimacy of our tight embrace. "I loved it."

"I love *you*," Kalun replied, unguardedly.

I lifted my head and gazed at him with enduring affection. "I love you too, Kalun. Now and forever."

We continued to hold each other close. Words were no longer necessary.

Later, after cleaning ourselves up and changing the soaked sheets, we once again collapsed into each other's arms.

It felt blissful to be in Kalun's warm embrace, yet a part of my mind couldn't help feeling unnerved by the prospect of the raid tomorrow.

I remembered what my mother used to say to me as a girl when I was fearful of the future, "Yesterday is history, tomorrow is a mystery, but today is a gift — that's why it's called the present".

As sleep crept up to claim my fatigued body and mind, I gave thanks for the gift of Kalun's pure and abiding love.

Chapter Ten

At first I thought I was dreaming.

Shouts and screams echoed around me.

Reality slowly emerged from deep unconsciousness.

My eyes shot open — it was pitch black in the cabin. I was disoriented and groggy.

I heard a crashing sound outside, then felt a heavy thud against the wall of the cabin.

I sat bolt upright, alarmed.

Kalun was stirring beside me.

He had heard the ominous noises too, which confirmed I hadn't been dreaming.

"What's going on out there?" I whispered urgently.

Kalun's eyes were wide with shock and confusion.

"I don't know…" he trailed off, then quickly swung his giant legs over the side of the bed.

He sprang over to the window and drew back the drapes.

Kalun released a gasp of panic, causing me to shoot out of the bed, but his giant frame was blocking my view of the outside.

"What is it? What's wrong?" I held my breath, fearing the response.

Kalun gave me a reluctant glance over his shoulder. He opened his mouth to say something but must have thought better of it, because he quickly clamped it shut again.

Something terrible was going on out there. The screams and the thumping sounds were growing louder and more terrifying.

I rushed to Kalun's side and gazed outside.

I took in a scene that would live with me until my dying day.

Chaos and destruction were unfolding right before my eyes.

Monstrous ogres were thundering through the village — maiming, killing, destroying. Burning cabins illuminated the horrifying view.

The ogres' grunts were loud, their giant feet pounded into the ground as they rampaged, destroying anything and everything in their path.

Some wielded enormous spiked clubs while others carried large burning torches, setting fire to dwellings and any other structures they came across.

I saw one ogre swinging his torch over his head and launching it onto the roof of a nearby cabin — I prayed the inhabitants had fled already.

Collective screams filled the air, turning my blood cold.

Just outside our cabin, villagers were shouting desperately to one another as they tried to scramble to safety, looking bewildered and blurry-eyed.

Mothers with their babies and young ones in their arms ran in all directions, attempting to flee the death and destruction.

I saw a little girl of about four standing on her own in the middle of the central square, looking bewildered and clutching a stuffed toy, while chaos reigned around her. She had been separated from her parents and was now a sitting duck.

Villagers were screaming. Mothers were wailing in fear. Young ones were bawling.

A barrage of lit torches went flying through the air, landing on homes and storage cabins, setting them ablaze in orange fireballs within seconds. Orc guards in full battle dress bravely barreled into the melee, swinging their weapons.

The scene was utter madness.

I glanced to my right. Kalun wasn't standing beside me anymore.

I'd been so transfixed by the horror unfolding outside that I hadn't realized what he was doing.

He had quickly dressed in his battle armor. As our eyes met, he looked at the scene outside, almost remorsefully.

"I have to help them out there," he said.

I nodded. "I know." He didn't need to explain himself to me.

"You need to run," he instructed, his eyes frantic as they locked with mine once again.

"Run…where?" My chest felt like it was collapsing.

Just minutes ago, we were sleeping soundly, cuddled up in the warmth of each other's arms. Now, our lives — and that of every other villager — were in the balance, in almost the blink of an eye.

"You need to get to the forest," shouted Kalun, as he grabbed his weapons from the living area. "Run as fast as you can and go as deep as you need to, until you cannot hear screaming."

I threw on my tunic and followed Kalun into the main room.

"I don't want to leave you," I said.

Kalun swung his burly body around. His eyes were wide with panic. I had never seen him so flustered.

"Hana…*please*." His voice was urgent.

I nodded. "Okay…I'll do it. I'll go to the forest." This was no time to argue.

Kalun reached for his helmet and placed it on his head.

"It is necessary for your safety," he said. "Once this is all—"

"They must have seen you," I cut in, suddenly hit by the awful realization. "At the ogre caves. It was my worst fear — that somehow the ogres caught sight of you and Vakar."

Kalun stared at me for a moment. His chest rose and fell rapidly.

"There is not much we can do to change that now," he said, grimly.

He hastily rushed to my side and cupped his fingers around my arm. "Come," he guided. "We must make haste. Flames could engulf the cabin at any moment."

He tugged me along towards the front door.

Once we were there, he abruptly stopped and quickly reached down to cradle my chin in his hands. He stared profoundly into my eyes, burning a hole in my soul with his gaze.

He roped me towards him and pressed me to his hard, massive chest, squeezing me tight, as if he was afraid this might be the last time he got to see me, hold me, touch me.

I surrendered completely to his embrace, lost in the moment. I wanted to memorize the smell of his skin, his tender touch, the ruggedness of his torso pressed up against my body.

"Be brave, my love," he said, urgently.

I knew he was trying to reassure me, but it was difficult to be positive when the sounds of screaming and destruction ripped through the air — and wasn't this chaos due to me? Because of *my* rescue? The thought was absolutely unbearable.

Kalun opened the door.

The smell of acrid smoke assaulted my senses. The loud cacophony of screams jarred my mind. Bodies were strewn on the ground. High flames licked the air. It was a scene from the most hellish of nightmares.

Kalun quickly led me down the steps before pointing towards the forest line.

"RUN!" he shouted, above the din of destruction.

I stood and watched as Kalun charged full-steam ahead to join his warriors at the forefront of the battle. Everything, including his movements, seemed to be occurring in slow, fragmented motions.

Kalun barreled into the belly of the action, his muscular legs propelling him swiftly. He gave a final glance over his shoulder, seeing me rooted to the spot. He pointed urgently towards the forest.

GO! — I read the word on his lips, but I couldn't hear him over the cries and shouting.

As soon as I saw that desperate command from him, it was like a kick in the back. I was on the move, running as fast as I could for the safety of the forest.

My thighs ached. My lungs burned. Tears welled in my eyes, blurring my vision and stinging my face. If I wanted to live, I had no choice but to flee the ogres' vengeful wrath.

The orcs had been horribly blindsided. I had no idea whether they would be a match for the monstrous ogres and their sheer brutality.

Fires burned around me, bodies lay in front of me and now the ground shook as a mammoth ogre fell nearby, taken down by the brave orc guards.

I leapt over the body of a poor orc female lying lifeless on the ground, a large gash on her temple, and finally made it to the edge of the forest.

I ran into the covering of trees and wild bushes. But instead of ploughing into the dense heart of the forest, I turned around and crouched down, finding cover behind thick brush. I felt compelled to witness the horrible scene.

My true love was putting his life on the line and the villagers, who had welcomed me with open arms, were fighting for survival. I could not simply bury myself in the forest, oblivious to their plight.

I scanned the village. Buildings burned. Civilians ran for the forest. Ogres trampled the dead, looking for more targets. Orc guards swung their ball and chains, defending their kin. Shouts and screams pierced the night.

My eyes fell on the central square. Standing there, still clutching her precious stuffed toy, was the same little girl I had spotted earlier. It was a miracle she had survived this long — but her chances were diminishing fast as flames licked the cabins nearby and ogres and orcs battled around her.

Swords clanked over her head. Spiked balls swung all around her. Yet she just stood there, unmoving, aside from her petrified green eyes — which feverishly darted left and right as if she were searching for something or someone. Her olive skin was covered with dirt and soot. Ash was peppered across her shoulders and sprinkled on her head. She looked like she had barely made it out of her cabin alive.

I desperately glanced around the area. I didn't see anyone around her that could be a parent, sibling or family member. No one appeared to be searching for her. She was truly alone.

I stood up. There was only one course of action.

This was not about my vows to nurture and protect all life

— this was about being able to live with myself for the rest of my days, however many I had left.

I put my head down and ran as fast as my legs would carry me directly towards the girl. I tried to block out any thoughts of the raging battle and focus only on the child. Miraculously, I met no obstacles on the way and reached her quickly.

I scooped her up in my arms. She looked so meek and scared, offering no resistance.

I turned around and headed back towards the forest, holding her tight to my chest.

I made slow progress. Orc youngsters are much heavier than their human equivalent and she was difficult to carry, but I managed the best I could, proceeding slowly but surely towards the safety of the trees.

Three-quarters of the way to the forest, I readjusted the girl in my arms to redistribute her weight — this was a huge mistake.

My forward motion combined with the shifting weight upset my balance. I tried to readjust, but to no avail. I stumbled, then fell to the ground, taking the child with me. Our legs and arms were sprawled out in front of us. The girl began crying. I wasn't sure if she was hurt or if it was just from the shock of the impact.

The girl continued to wail as I quickly crawled to her and tried to pick her back up. We were *so* close to safety now.

As I hooked my hands under her arms to lift her, the ground shook around us.

I looked up and my heart stopped in my chest.

To my horror, a mammoth ogre with deranged, dark eyes stood in front of us, blocking our path. He was caked in mud and ash, and carried a massive spiked club, which was horrifyingly covered with fresh crimson blood.

I held the girl protectively in my arms, staring up at the terrifying beast.

Realization flooded me — I *knew* this ogre.

This was the same monster who had taken me from the convent, tied me to a rock and planned to have his horde rape and murder me for 'sport'. Standing in front of me — his deadly club now raised high — was Tyrankreg-Gimtulan.

I tried to summon any courage I had left in my body and soul.

"Leave her alone…she is just a child," I shouted, raising myself to a standing position.

I moved the girl protectively behind my body, my arms roped backwards to hold her close.

"Take me." I met the gaze of the beast. "You only wanted me in the first place."

I was facing my end — I would fight to perform one last sisterly deed.

Tyrankreg-Gimtulan's wicked, black eyes danced with amusement. His gnarly lips curled into a deranged smile of delight. He roared with unhinged laughter — sickening globs of drool and spittle sprayed from his mouth and hit me in the face.

"It's the Queen Cunt herself," he declared. "This evening is now perfect."

He threw his head back and cackled manically once more.

While he did this I quickly went to my knees and turned to the girl. I placed my hands firmly on her shoulders and stared deep into her frightened eyes.

"Run for your life," I said simply, then pushed her forwards.

Mercifully, she sprang ahead and dodged around the laughing ogre before dashing for the tree line.

But once there, she didn't enter the forest. Instead, she turned around and simply stared at me, seemingly transfixed by my fate. I mentally urged her to run forward, to lose herself in the safety of the undergrowth. She did not budge. I couldn't shout to her, lest I reveal to Tyrankreg-Gimtulan that the girl had fled and was standing just behind him.

The best I could do was distract the ogre — with my own death. I hoped that after seeing me perish, the girl would have no reason to wait around and would finally seek safety.

"Do it then, beast," I raged. "This is the *only* manner in which you will have me."

I squared my shoulders, unyielding. I refused to show fear or cower in the face of this wicked animal. He would not dictate how I faced my end.

He raised his club higher over his head, a gleam of excitement in his wild eyes. His spiked weapon loomed intimidatingly over my head. I braced myself for the impact.

I wasn't ready to die, there was so much more I wanted to do — see my sisters freed, perhaps even settle with Kalun and have children — but it seemed that my road had run out.

I mentally recited the Absolution Rite.

Lord in Heaven have mercy on my soul. Forgive my sins and make me pure, so that I may enter your mighty kingdom...

The ogre's enormous club thundered down to strike my head.

My muscles seized. My mind went blank. Every sound, thought and fear was erased.

I squeezed my eyes shut. I didn't want the ogre's gruesome, hateful face to be the last image I saw before departing the mortal realm.

I waited. There was nothing else I could do. I was now in the hands of the Divine.

Oddly, I didn't feel any pain. I didn't feel the blow at all.

Is this how it was? Was the actual physical passing painless? Was it over? Was I dead?

I summoned enough fortitude to peel one eye slightly open.

What I saw made me gasp with shock.

Narag's massive body was on top of the ogre, who was now sprawled on the ground.

Miraculously, the orc leader must have tackled the giant beast just as the club came down, and now had him pinned to the ground.

Narag's arms and legs pounded into the ogre's body with violent rage — he must have lost his weapon earlier in the raid. He was grunting as he landed jabs and punches. His eyes were filled with fire and fury. Each fist he pummeled into the massive ogre was laced with anger. He gritted his teeth, groaning with rage.

My breath caught with alarm. With no weapon, what chance did Narag stand against Tyrankreg-Gimtulan, who was almost twice his size. The element of surprise had allowed the orc an advantage for now, but the massive ogre would soon regain his bearings.

"Get out of here, Hana," Narag shouted, through labored breaths. "HURRY — before it's too late."

I couldn't move. I was like a stone statue, unable to convince any part of my body to shift. I stared at Narag, who had come to my aid in what surely would have been the final moments of my life.

Narag was fighting for his life (and mine), but his efforts were failing him. The ogre started gaining the upper hand —

his arms and hands were twice the size of Narag's — and he was using them to devastating effect as he pummeled the orc's body.

Narag tried to scramble away, but the ogre was able to swiftly rise to a sitting position and grab his leg, dragging him back. The ogre pinned Narag's arms to the ground, so he couldn't fight back anymore.

Narag grimaced and squirmed in the ogre's grasp, but couldn't find a way to escape the steely grip of the enormous creature. He stared up at me, with desperation in his eyes.

"Hana, GO NOW!" he shouted.

I looked up and saw the girl still rooted to the spot just in front of the trees. That gave me the impetus to start moving.

The last thing I saw before fleeing was the ogre raising his giant fist and then crashing it down on the side of Narag's temple.

I watched in horror as Narag's eyes rolled back in his head.

I was desperate to assist him, but there was nothing I could do, and the girl was still in danger.

I ran to her and scooped her up in my arms. I hurtled towards the tree line with the terrified child.

Once we reached the woods, I kept going. It was like my legs had a mind of their own. I ripped through the tree branches and underbrush, heading deeper and deeper into the dense belly of the forest until the sounds of screaming receded.

When I finally stopped, I gently placed the girl down on the soft earth.

My legs felt like jelly. My heart was pounding ferociously. A wave of nausea crashed through my stomach.

I was so distraught that my vision blurred. I felt like my body might fail me at any moment. But I had to stay strong, for the girl. There was no guarantee we were out of danger.

Now that we had left the village — the only home she knew and where her loved-ones still were — the girl began crying loudly.

I cupped my hands around her shoulders and knelt to eye level with her.

"Shh, sweetie," I whispered in a low voice. "You must be brave. We are hiding from the ogres. We don't want them to find us, do we?"

The little girl vigorously shook her head. "No."

Her voice was a tiny little mouse squeak. My heart broke for her and the overwhelming fear she must be experiencing. I tenderly wiped the tears from her cheeks with my thumb.

"Everything is going to be okay," I tried to reassure. "I will help you find your mommy and daddy again. I promise."

The little girl had captivating green eyes. She stared at me, hanging on to every word I said.

I hated to make promises that I wasn't confident I could keep, but I needed to calm her down and give her some kind of hope to cling to.

"Come here," I whispered.

I embraced her in a tight hug and rubbed her back, dusting the ash from her shoulders.

"Shh…don't cry. You are safe now. The ogres can't find us here. This is our safe place."

"I'm scared," the girl admitted, her voice cracking.

"I know, but we must be brave — like the warriors in the village. We must be like them."

As I said the words, I tried my best to heed my own advice, but it was difficult.

My mind kept replaying the last desperate shout from Narag

to me, the final look of agony in his anxious eyes.

I also thought of Kalun — I didn't know if he was alive or dead at this point.

If I closed my eyes, I could still feel the warmth of his embrace. His sturdy body pressed up against mine. There was every chance that I would be left with only memories now.

I cradled the crying child in my arms, rocking her back and forth, praying for the village and all the souls who dwelled there.

The girl let out a whimper. I couldn't even begin to imagine the emotional turmoil she must be feeling, being ripped from slumber and frantically fleeing her burning home, torn from her parents and now in the arms of a strange human in the dark, dense forest. I held her close.

***

After a while, I could no longer hear cries of distress, nor the crackle of flames devouring wood. It was eerily, hauntingly quiet.

The child was quivering in my arms from the cold.

I stood up and slowly carried her back towards the edge of the forest.

"Don't make a sound," I instructed. "Not until I can be certain we are out of harm's way."

The girl nodded her understanding and shivered in my arms.

As we reached the tree line, I stopped, ducked down and looked out.

I saw ruin.

Cabins and buildings had turned to ash, some with nothing left but the foundations, some gone all together. Small fires still burned here and there.

The surviving orcs were tending to the wounded and dead.

It was heartbreaking to witness the carnage as my eyes scrolled the landscape.

The village was in a dreadful state, but the ogres seemed to have dissipated, content that they had wreaked enough damage and claimed enough lives to exact their brutal revenge.

Satisfied that the threat had receded, I slowly stood and led the girl by the hand back to the village. Once there, we turned in a slow circle to scan our surroundings.

An orc female stood a few feet away from us, alone and looking devastated. She was wearing a pastel blue gown that had been ripped at the shoulder. It was caked with dirt and the bottom edges of it were scorched from fire. Her face was streaked with tears.

"Mommy!" the child shouted, wiggling her body, attempting to free herself from my grip.

As soon as the child called out for her, the orc collapsed to her knees. All strength had left her body. She stared wide-eyed before holding out trembling arms.

The girl barreled into her embrace.

The mother hooked her arms around her child, sobbing and holding her so tight as if to convince herself she was real. My eyes flooded with tears.

Among the utter devastation, this was one ray of hope.

My joy was short-lived.

The still night was shattered by a scream of heartbreak.

I turned towards the sound.

Sherrine was standing a few yards away from me. Her posture was crumpled. Her shoulders were shaking with grief.

I made my way to her side, with dread lodged in my heart.

Sherrine held her precious baby Armaan in her arms, rocking him back and forth. A crowd was beginning to form around them.

As I got closer, I realized that Sherrine was standing beside a body slumped on the ground.

Nya was by Sherrine's side, trying to calm her down, stroking her back, whispering to her.

Sherrine was sobbing inconsolably, and tiny Armaan was wailing in response to his mother's crippling anguish.

The body on the ground — I knew all too well — was that of Narag.

My heart stopped. I felt like someone had just swiftly kicked me in the gut, knocking the air from my lungs. The world began to spin.

Sherrine collapsed to her knees, taking the baby with her.

Nya quickly reached down for Armaan. Sherrine released him from her grasp, almost absentmindedly.

Sherrine's focus was on the unmoving orc. She reached her arms around to hug Narag's massive body, continuing to cry with endless sorrow.

My heart broke into a million pieces for her. There were simply no words.

Fat tears stained Armaan's cheeks and he gasped for air, wailing and squirming harder now. Nya had to struggle to control him.

Sherrine pressed her face into Narag's lifeless torso, weeping for his departed soul.

Guilt slammed into me. Narag had been trying to save *me*

when he died. The attack on the village was due to *my* rescue. *I* was the root cause of this death and destruction.

I was poison. I was cursed. Death stalked me — cruelly taking those around me — while taunting me with undeserving life.

Narag's death was a burden I would carry for the rest of my life — a life which I did not deserve. I looked up at the now fatherless Armaan, distraught and uncomprehending in Nya's arms.

My legs failed me. My knees gave way. I collapsed to the ground beside Sherrine. I clutched her shoulder and cried along with her. My eyes burned. Tears rolled down my cheeks. I felt so empty inside.

Large hands wrapped themselves around my waist and pulled me to a standing position.

I turned around — it was Kalun — he was alive.

I should have felt elated, but I simply collapsed with despair into his arms.

He was holding me up, my legs would not bear my weight.

"You cannot blame yourself," he soothed into my ear. "It is not your fault. Do not dare blame yourself, Hana."

It wasn't true. I beat my hands against his chest, rejecting his words.

He tightened his embrace, so my arms couldn't flail into him

"Narag died an honorable death," he said. "That is what we hope for as warriors. His legacy will be spoken—

"I did this," I cut in, angrily. "All of this."

"You are not at fault," Kalun replied, burying his head into my shoulder. "You are *not* at fault."

He could tell me a million times over that I wasn't to blame. It would make no difference to my guilt-stricken conscience.

My previous thought returned to me with full force — *I am poison... I am poison... I am poison... I am poison...*

Chapter Eleven

I didn't want to ever venture outside the seclusion of Kalun's cabin.

I wanted to hide away here forever in shame.

I felt like I was the cause of the horror inflicted against the orc village.

All around, death and destruction served as a visceral reminder of everything that had been lost.

Every gutted home and hastily-built funeral pyre was another stab to my heart. No matter how fervently Kalun tried to convince me otherwise, I carried the weight of remorse heavily on my shoulders.

As if the world was in mourning too, a blanket of hazy fog cloaked the village in the aftermath of the attack.

The fog stretched out across the horizon, as far as the eye could see. The sky was a dismal gray color and a cold, damp mist spread across the landscape, almost as if the Heavens were weeping alongside us.

"Cremations will take place for the dead all day," Kalun

explained somberly, his emotions numb, making him difficult to read. "Narag's will be the final one, in the evening."

I nodded my understanding, remaining stoically silent for most of the breaking dawn.

I wanted to stay out of the way. I felt like I didn't belong here. I wanted to give these poor orcs their privacy to grieve and wrap themselves in each other's comfort and solace.

I wanted to give them space, even Kalun — although he was fighting me every step of the way. I felt like I didn't deserve the love and sympathy he was so vehemently trying to give to me.

"You will be attending most of the cremations, I assume, due to your position?" I asked, gazing up at him with a pitifully bleak expression.

Kalun nodded grimly, then gave me a softer glance.

"I am still hoping that you will accompany me," he said.

I shifted my focus to my lap, my shoulders wilting.

I wasn't intentionally trying to wallow in pity, but my raw emotions wouldn't allow me to act in any other way.

Kalun walked to where I was sitting on the bed and knelt to eye level with me. He stroked my cheek and lifted my chin, forcing me to look into his concerned eyes.

"Say it with me," he coaxed, gently. "It is not your fault."

I lowered my head and continued staring at my lap.

He exhaled deeply and wrapped my small hands in his.

"When I was at my lowest, you made me see sense," he said, gently. "I hope I can do the same for you."

I looked up into his sympathetic eyes again.

"Think about it," he encouraged. "You did not ask to be rescued from the ogres. It is a decision *we* made — Vakar, Nya and me. You are blameless here. If anything, I am at fault for not having dispatched the ogre guarding you cleanly. He was able to raise the alarm, then we must have been seen. I am—"

"Don't," I cut in, sternly, squeezing his hands. "*None* of this is your doing, Kalun. You have only ever tried to do the right thing."

"Then say it," he implored. "For me."

I took a deep breath, finding strength in his compassionate gaze.

"It's not…" my voice cracked and I couldn't complete the rest of the statement without my eyes flooding with fat tears.

"Take a deep breath and close your eyes," Kalun said, cupping his hands over my shoulders and squeezing them gently. "One more time, Hana."

"It's not…my…fault." I made it through, but barely.

When I opened my eyes again, Kalun was giving me a compassionate smile. He was so good to me, my rock, my anchor in the storm.

He traced his hands down to my arms then slowly lifted me to a standing position.

"Come with me today," he encouraged. "I know what it is like to lock yourself away, fearing the outside world. No good comes of it."

"I…I'm not sure," I mumbled, apprehensively.

He cupped my chin in his giant hands.

"One step at a time, my love," he reassured. "If at any time you feel overwhelmed, then the safety of these walls are always here for you."

I took a deep breath and nodded at him, hesitantly.

"One step at a time," I repeated, searching his warm eyes for reassurance.

I changed my tunic and splashed cold water on my face

before accompanying Kalun outside.

Dawn light infused the hazy fog with an ethereal quality, bathing the landscape in a warm orange glow.

My heart sank as I took in the cremation pyres dotted throughout the village. Mourning family members — young and old — huddled around fallen mothers, fathers, sons and daughters, paying their final respects.

My eyes fell on a small huddle of orcs close to us, who were gathered around a makeshift pyre of wood and dried leaves. I couldn't make out the deceased as a grieving female was blocking the view, her head resting on the body as she wailed in despair.

A male family member gently pulled her away — and then my heart collapsed.

Lying on the dry foliage, looking angelic — almost as if he were simply taking a brief nap — was a small boy, his arms draped peacefully on his chest. In his hands was a small doll made from stuffed cloth. His family wanted him to have something familiar to bring him comfort as his spirit journeyed on.

I was overcome with sorrow — but also burning rage. How could the ogres be so merciless as to claim innocent children? It was beyond my comprehension.

Kalun noticed me staring and gently coaxed me along.

We spent most of the day making our way around the various cremations, paying our heartfelt respects to family members of the departed.

I mostly stood to Kalun's side, feeling awkward and out of place. However, I did not flee for the refuge of the cabin. I couldn't simply run and hide while he endured the burden alone.

As we continued on our grim tour, I couldn't help noticing how well respected Kalun was within the community. Villagers openly wept in his arms.

He consoled each and every family member of the fallen — women, children, brothers, sisters, mothers, fathers, uncles, aunts — anyone who needed a shoulder to cry on or a few words of solace. He offered his time and attention without a moment's hesitation.

Kalun ensured we didn't skip over a single grieving soul in the village. He made the effort to stop at each cremation site and speak, however briefly, to all the mourners.

By the time we returned to his cabin in the afternoon, I was drained both physically and emotionally. In all honesty, I was practically falling apart. My emotions were raw and frayed after witnessing so much grief, so much senseless death. Guilt still weighed me down. My heart was filled with sorrow at the sheer scale of the loss.

Kalun walked over to a seat in the living area and sat down heavily, looking fatigued and emotionally drained.

I approached him from behind and began rubbing his broad shoulders, attempting to offer some relief from the tension I knew he felt, because I felt it too.

"That was almost unbearable," I confided. "I don't know how we are going to make it through Narag's cremation ceremony this evening."

Kalun cleared his throat and paused a moment.

"It is going to be very difficult," he finally said, in a low voice that was laced with heartbreak.

I wanted to comfort him, but I couldn't find the right words. There were no appropriate words for the depth of loss. All I could do was rub his shoulders and stroke his back, to give him some physical reassurance that he was not alone in this moment.

"We could try to get some rest," I suggested. "That might be beneficial for our bodies and spirits."

Kalun nodded, almost absentmindedly. "Okay."

"We don't have to if you don't want to…" I trailed off.

Kalun lifted his gaze and turned towards me. It tore my soul to see how red-rimmed and bloodshot his eyes were. They were a window into his unrelenting sorrow.

"No, it is a wise suggestion," he said in an exhausted voice. "I think rest is what we need."

I took his hand and drew him to a standing position. We retreated to the bedroom and lay down, staring up at the ceiling, hand in hand. Neither of us uttered a word for a while.

"Narag and the others died as innocents, uncorrupted," I said, finally. "They will reach Heaven — this is our belief."

I hoped my words could offer a measure of solace and help ease his mind — mine also, to be completely truthful.

"I'm sure Narag has already gained his wings, and is soaring through the skies," I continued. "He will always look out for the village, and…" I trailed off as my voice broke. "His beloved Sherrine and Armaan."

I couldn't bear to think of the poor little baby, who would now have to grow up without a father. It was brutally, devastatingly unfair.

"I wish it could have been me instead," Kalun said, turning his head towards me.

"Don't talk like that, Kalun," I said, alarmed.

"*I* wasn't a father," Kalun stated. "Too many young ones will be going to sleep tonight without a father or mother."

I lifted his hand to my heart and squeezed it tight.

"You can't carry the burden of everyone's pain," I implored, even though the words felt hollow as soon as they left my lips. How could I give him that advice when I couldn't even convince myself?

I held him close, thankful for this brief moment of respite. We lay in silence. There was nothing left to say. Finally, we succumbed to the blissful oblivion of sleep, where we didn't ache with every fiber of our body and soul.

***

I drifted out of a deep, dreamless slumber. My eyes fluttered open.

It was early evening. The sun hadn't gone down completely, but it was visibly darker in the cabin than it had been earlier.

I glanced to Kalun's side of the bed. He wasn't lying beside me.

My heart jumped into my throat. For a moment my groggy mind thought he had perished in the raid.

I sat bolt upright and urgently scanned the room.

Relief flooded over me.

Kalun was standing at the end of the bed.

"What are you doing?" I asked, my galloping heartbeat finally slowing down.

Kalun's face was partially hidden in shadows, partially glowing under the light of several candles that he had lit around the room. As my eyes slowly adjusted, I could see he was putting on his battle armor.

"Getting ready," Kalun said in a monotone voice, staring

straight ahead.

"It is customary for the guard to dress in full battle attire during the ceremony for a fellow warrior," he explained. "Plus Narag was our village chief."

I exhaled heavily. This was going to be a difficult evening for all involved.

"I can't even imagine how crushed Sherrine must be feeling," I said.

"Hopeless, I imagine," Kalun said, turning to face me, his expression grim.

"I wish there was something I could do or say to her," I admitted. "But everything I think of simply falls short."

Kalun's expression softened.

"You can be there for her," he said. "That is all you can do, and that is what she needs right now, just to feel she is not alone."

I nodded and climbed out of bed, drifting slowly to where Kalun stood at the end of the room. I cuffed my hand around his big forearm and gave it a gentle squeeze before stroking it affectionately. Kalun let out a breath and eyed me with empathy.

He reached out to stroke my cheek with a tenderness I felt I didn't deserve.

I felt guilty experiencing comfort, consolation and warmth, while so many were suffering.

"We had better finish getting ready," Kalun said, with a hint of hesitation, as if he wasn't prepared to say goodbye to his loyal friend and leader. "The entire village will be in attendance."

We quickly dressed and left the cabin, hand in hand for mutual support, and made our way to the central square, where we weaved our way through the dense crowd of villagers.

Hearts were heavy. Faces were stoic and somber. Some were crying softly, their eyes red and swollen, their cheeks stained with old and fresh tears.

A palpable cloud of sorrow hung over the village, enveloping every one of us.

Dusk was settling over the landscape, reflecting the sadness in our hearts.

Once we reached the front, Kalun and I discreetly stepped beside Sherrine, who was holding baby Armaan. Nya and Vakar, who stood on the other side of her, provided meager smiles as we approached.

Nya was standing beside Sherrine on the left, and I took up position to her right. Without having to say a word, we were determined to surround Sherrine with our sisterly love and support. Just behind us stood a row of orc warriors in their full battle dress. Vakar and Kalun stepped back to fall in line with their comrades.

Behind them, it appeared the entire village was in attendance. Rows and rows of orcs, young and old, had come to pay their respects to their courageous leader, who had given his life to defend those under his care.

Flames from burning torches illuminated the scene as darkness enveloped the landscape.

Narag's body was lying on ornately carved wooden planks atop the large funeral pyre. He was dressed in his finest battle armor. His eyes were closed. If you didn't know any better, you might think he was just sleeping peacefully. He looked gallant, regal even, in his final repose. Dried flowers were scattered around his large body.

Sherrine stepped forwards, little Armaan held close to her chest. Tears streaked her pale cheeks as she approached the body. Her shoulders began to shake with grief.

Baby Armaan reached out for his father. He waved his tiny green fists at Narag, his features etched with both joy and confusion upon seeing his father.

"Da-da," Armaan babbled excitedly, leaning over to pat his father on the chest. "Da-da…da-da…"

He drummed his hands on his father again when he received no response.

"Da-da…play?…" Armaan squeaked, frowning, his eyes wide with bemusement.

Silence was the only response.

The poor baby became increasingly distraught the longer his father went without answering him.

"Da-da…*play?*…" Armaan implored, his voice breaking.

Huge, fat tears welled in his big brown eyes and rolled down his cheeks.

"Da-da…*play*," he insisted harder, shaking Narag fervently with his two small hands.

Of course, Narag would never respond, but that was difficult for Armaan to comprehend.

"Da-da…*up*," Armaan cried. He pounded his tiny, balled fist onto Narag's unmoving, unbreathing chest. "Da-da…*up*…."

"Shh…" Sherrine whispered, attempting to sooth her distraught baby. "It's okay. Daddy is with you…he will *always* be with you." She buried her face in the child's mop of brown curls and wept for their shared loss.

"Da-da…sleep?" Armaan asked, craning his neck to give Sherrine a puzzled glance.

Sherrine nodded her head gingerly. She brushed tears from her baby's cheeks. Her eyes glistened with wetness. Her voice cracked. "Yes, baby…da-da is very tired…he needs to sleep now," she trailed off, crying harder.

She began slowly stepping backwards, away from the body.

As she did, Armaan began crying harder and louder. His heartbreaking sounds of sorrow rang out across the entire village. The baby roared and wailed, reaching his arms out for his father as he was carried away.

"Da-da...*play*..." Armaan howled, arms outstretched. "Da-da...*up*...da-da...*play*..."

It was simply devastating to watch the tragic scene unfold.

Sherrine kept walking backwards, increasing the gap between Armaan and Narag.

"Shh," she tried to console the squirming Armaan, her face red and blotchy with grief. "Da-da has to sleep now, baby."

Armaan's features were etched with confusion and anguish as he was separated from his unmoving father.

He continued staring wide-eyed at Narag, as if he fully expected him to sit up and reach out for him, to smile and wrap his baby up in his strong, consoling arms.

None of that would happen, but how could you explain such things to an infant already gripped by misery?

"Da-da...da-da..." Armaan whimpered, his voice cracked. It seemed all strength had left his small body. He clung tightly to his mother's neck while pleading over and over again: "Da-da...*up*... da-da...*up*..."

I had to look away. It was too much for my soul to bear.

I glanced back at Kalun and the row of guards. These were hardened warriors who had seen the horrors of battle — not one face wasn't streaked with tears.

Kalun's chin quivered with grief while Vakar didn't even attempt to wipe the tears off his cheeks. It was simply impossible to hear the tortured infant begging for his father to wake up and not react with sorrow, even for the toughest and most resilient fighter.

Sherrine turned around, facing the crowd.

She squared her shoulders and straightened her posture, handing over the sobbing Armaan to Nya, who attempted to pacify him as best as she could.

Sherrine took a deep breath to compose herself.

In the midst of her misery and heartbreak, to me she still looked beautiful, so naturally radiant. She was also so strong. I admired her for even being able to get out of bed, much less give a speech in front of the entire village.

She didn't crumble or collapse. She held herself together, stoic and resolved — just like Narag. He would have been so proud of her.

"We are gathered here today to mourn the loss of a father, a warrior, a leader and my beloved," she said.

Sherrine paused. Sniffles and cries hummed through the crowd. Bleak faces blinked up at her.

"He died as he lived," she continued. "In the service of others, putting the needs of the many in front of his own. Though he wasn't one to readily show his emotions, he cared deeply for each and every one of you and considered you all his family..." Sherrine trailed off and looked away, her voice breaking.

She paused again to collect herself. More sniffles and sobs were heard through the crowd.

"Narag was the most honorable soul I have ever met. He spent his life trying to make sure that the weak were protected and justice and fairness were received by all."

She stopped to give her baby an adoring smile.

"His spirit lives on in our little Armaan, who he cherished more than anything in this world. His son carries within him the love and compassion that made Narag so special. I will ensure that his legacy lives on in Armaan's words and deeds. He will be raised to know his father's abiding truth: that strong people stand up for themselves — stronger people stand up for others."

There wasn't a single dry eye as the attention shifted to Armaan, now lying still in Nya's loving embrace. More sobbing echoed through the crowd.

Sherrine took another deep breath. "So let us all ensure that Narag did not die in vain, that his legacy lives on in all our hearts. Let us be a light in each other's lives. Let us care for one another, and give succor and service to those in need. Let us protect those who do not have a voice, or who are too weak to defend themselves. It is the creed by which Narag lived by — and the very best way we can honor his memory."

The crowd erupted, clapping, cheering, crying.

Sherrine stepped aside, taking her baby back from Nya.

The two women hugged, consoling each other with the baby in between them. I rubbed Sherrine's back and kissed tiny Armaan on the cheek while stroking his soft brown curls.

After a brief pause, the tribal priest came to the front, carrying a burning torch. He wore long white robes and had an ornate headdress made from bird feathers. His face was covered in a swirling tattoo and his neck was adorned with countless necklaces, each one with a wooden pendant in the shape of an astrological symbol.

He began reciting an incantation in the orc dialect.

"Eshtalar-ethrallune di cantak, ethrallune mara di mithraldin, naresh eshtar di tithlanad — Tarek da sharant."

"Tarek da sharant," the entire village repeated in unison.

"The soul has departed the body, but lives on in the eternal.

What was never ours can never be taken away," the priest translated.

The crowd was silent as he took the torch and gently rested it against the dry kindling on the corner of the pyre.

Immediately, the flames began to spread, engulfing the kindling and small branches first, then spreading to the dry leaves before reaching the wooden planks. Finally the orange fire lit up Narag's body, sending flames high into the dark sky.

Armaan wailed so hard that Sherrine had to bury his face into her chest.

The huge blaze danced skywards, reaching high into night, as if transporting Narag's soul to the Heavens.

Embers fluttered like snowflakes to the ground below, settling across the landscape, as well as dusting our shoulders and heads. We simply stood there, allowing the ash to fall freely on us, somehow feeling that we were bathed in Narag's noble spirit.

I gazed hypnotically at the fierce flames which, like Narag himself, would burn bright — but be gone all too soon.

Chapter Twelve

I was awoken from deep slumber by the ominous sounds of voices and activity outside.

It was dark and I had an alarming sense of deja vu.

It was hard to determine what was causing the commotion, but the unrest was growing louder with each passing moment.

Fear lodged in my heart. I was seized by debilitating panic.

I didn't want to jump to conclusions, but I was sure the ogres must have returned — to kick us while we were down and finish us off once and for all.

"Kalun?" I hissed into the darkness. "Kalun! Do you hear the noises outside?"

"Yes," he replied instantaneously, then shot out of bed and swiftly moved to the window.

"What's going on out there?" I whispered, feeling overwhelmed by shock.

"There's a disturbance, but I cannot make out what," he said, his voice laced with unmistakable fear.

"Could it be ogres?" I asked as Kalun reached for his battle armor, which he now kept by his bedside when sleeping.

"We will soon find out," he replied, urgently. "Get dressed, Hana. We must vacate the cabin *now*."

He didn't need to tell me twice. The horrific images of burning dwellings were still fresh in my mind.

We threw our clothes on and headed for the front door.

"Stay behind me at all times," Kalun instructed, protecting me with his brawny body as we left the cabin.

He took my hand and guided me warily out into the night.

A handful of orc guards were standing at the perimeter of the village, where it met the forest, clutching burning torches tight in their fists.

After the first ogre attack, guards had been placed at various points around the outskirts of the village, to keep watch and raise the alarm in case of another attack.

Tensions were still running sky high following the devastating raid.

I could see in the distance that the guards were clustered around one particular point near the forest edge. I narrowed my eyes to try to make out what was going on.

I suddenly froze — incapacitated by deep-seated dread. I could just make out a cluster of huge, unidentifiable creatures slowly emerging from the forest.

Kalun stopped abruptly in his tracks.

We just stood there and stared at the unfolding scene.

More of the large creatures emerged from the trees.

"They…they…don't look big enough to be ogres…" I trailed off, straining my eyes to look closer at the group.

"It is hard to tell from this vantage point," Kalun replied.

"But they are too big to be orcs," I said, gripped by confusion and fear.

What kind of new threat was this? What were these strange creatures? Did they mean us harm?

At least they had not attacked — yet.

Kalun slowly edged closer to the group. I followed in his footsteps, keeping my body concealed behind him. I peeked out every so often, scoping the dark landscape with apprehension.

"Stay close to me," Kalun advised over his shoulder.

I nodded as we approached the group with a few more guards gathering at our sides.

As we got close enough to make out the details of the intruders, I realized, with open-mouthed surprise, that I had been wrong — these *were* orcs. But unlike any I had ever seen before. They were huge in comparison to the orcs in the village, at least a full head and shoulders taller.

The new orcs brooded over us with the same distrust and wariness that we were showing them.

They were bare-chested but wore leather coverings around their waists and straps around their wrists. They had sculpted physiques, with massive chests and bicep muscles that resembled boulders. The rippled abdominal muscles on their torsos looked like mini grooves chiseled out of stone. They had the same olive complexions but, as they leered at us with intimidating scowls, I noticed large, sharp canine teeth in their mouths.

Another striking difference was they had hair — and lots of it. The males from the village were mostly all bald. The newcomers' hair was jet black and worn in a slicked-back, mohawk style with a long braid trailing behind their backs.

They carried enormous battle hammers made of granite — a weapon that I had never seen orcs wield before. The heads of hammers looked worn and well-used, sending a shudder of dread through my body. I didn't want to even imagine the damage these gruesome weapons could inflict on a victim.

They stared at us, sizing us up with judgmental stares.

Kalun moved into a protective stance in front of me. He took a deep breath and puffed out his chest to signify that we were not cowed and would not acquiesce easily, but the mysterious orcs paid him no heed. They didn't seem intimidated or concerned by the presence of our warriors, not in the slightest.

There was a discordant energy in the air and I had the feeling that things could turn violent at any moment.

I had no idea what was going on and where they had come from or — most critically — what they wanted from us, especially in the dead of night.

The orcs at the front of their troop were somewhat restrained, but the rows in the back were now whistling, jeering and pushing towards the front, with wild eyes and loud chants of *"Kallak-Edah...Kallak-Edah...Kallak-Edah...Kallak-Edah..."*

This was obviously a battle cry — which did not bode well at all.

The biggest orc in the group stepped forward, his intimidating war hammer raised high in his hand. Deep scars crisscrossed his wide chest and I noticed he was the only one wearing a pendant around his neck. It was carved of metal and in the shape of a bird of prey, its talons stretched out to claim a kill.

His eyes prowled our line of guards with a smug, condescending sneer spread across his lips. His aura was practically bleedingarrogance.

He had a callous expression, showing his indifference to the fact that he was disrupting a sleeping, mourning village in the middle of the night.

His fractious crew continued to shout and holler behind him.

More light began to illuminate the scene as villagers carried lanterns outside.

I looked behind me and saw orcs gathered in the night, families huddled together protectively, escaping the potential danger of their cabins. Though they eyed the commotion with interest, they wisely opted to keep their distance.

The lead orc scanned the crowd of assembled villagers with a menacing sneer. He held his shoulders high and his posture was proud, dominating. I caught a glimpse of Kalun out of the corner of my eye. He was glaring fixedly at the orc in question.

"I am Darrakh of the Ukangher tribe," bellowed the leader, his voice deep and tone imperious. "I come here tonight accompanied by my warriors to make a declaration to all of you — a declaration that if you had any sense or respect for our ancestry you would already have known was coming."

I stepped closer to Kalun, gripping his arm, as this Darrakh took a moment to scan everyone around him, ensuring he had our full, undivided attention.

"Regarding the ogre attack on your village," he continued. "It has come to our attention that during the raid you were weak and did little to defend yourselves. You lacked courage. You lacked fighting spirit. You let these filthy beasts rampage through your village, allowing them free reign to do as they pleased."

He raised his hand and pointed a finger, sweeping it in an arc across the entire village.

"You Sherrakh-Shen are a disgrace to our noble ancestry and shared bloodline. Your cowardice and gutlessness now put every orc clan in the land in danger. Because of your spineless display, you have sent an open invitation to any and all creatures of the night to take our lands, to slay our females and young ones."

My mouth was agape. I couldn't believe what I was hearing.

Darrakh paused for effect, his eyes roaming the crowd with disdain, waiting for someone to argue against him. I could tell that he loved drama, directing intimidation and contempt at those he viewed as beneath him. He wanted to get a rise out of us.

I warily tossed a glance at our warrior guard — still standing proudly in opposition to his horde. Kalun's jaw was tight with anger. His eyes flickered with fury. His fists were balled at his sides as he gave a death stare to Darrakh.

Anxiety settled into my stomach, making me slightly queasy.

I dreaded another battle. We couldn't afford to lose any more lives, to shed any more blood. I didn't think our spirits could take it. We were already crushed by so much loss and sorrow.

None of our guards contested Darrakh — but they didn't hang their heads in shame, either. Their faces were etched with defiance and resolve. Their blood was up and it wouldn't take much for this powder keg of animosity to explode. I could feel the hostility practically reverberating through the air.

When Darrakh didn't receive any initial protests, he continued.

"We need strong, fearless orcs to ensure the survival of the generations yet to come — not pathetic cowards who would capitulate in the face of confrontation. We Ukangher share our heritage with you Sherrakh-Shen, which makes me sick to my stomach."

His face contorted with disgust.

"By association, our honorable name has been dragged through the mud on account of your action…" Darrakh trailed off and his pompous smirk made a reappearance. "Or…*lack* of action, I might say."

His troops jeered behind him. I counted roughly forty in all.

Darrakh took another pause, flexing his huge biceps and giving us a look of utter contempt through narrowed eyes.

"After revealing your weakness, your deficiency, the Ukangher are here to claim your village — as is our right under the ancestral laws. We hereby give notice that we are taking your land, your resources and your females."

Darrakh's eyes wandered over the guards and villagers. They stopped on me. His lips curled into a smarmy smile. I shivered and looked at the ground, feeling violated by his probing stare.

Kalun coiled his arm around my waist and squeezed me tightly before reaching for my hand, all the while continuing to stare at Darrakh with undisguised hostility.

"If you were smart — which apparently you are *not* judging by your slack-jawed expressions— you would have already seen this coming," declared Darrakh. "It is our sacred right to claim this village by well-established custom. Weakness must be eliminated and cowardice punished — for the greater good of the bloodline. This is our way. This is the price you must pay for disgrace and dishonor."

Darrakh's voice thundered through the village.

I looked around at the villagers. Worried faces stared fixedly at Darrakh, hanging on his every word.

"Who here *dares* to stand in our way?" challenged Darrakh. "Probably none of you — because cowering at the first sign of trouble is in your pitiful nature."

More jeers rang out among his followers.

It was clear that Darrakh was looking for a reaction — any kind of reaction — from the village, and particularly from the orc guards.

He wanted someone to defy him so he could make a quick example out of them. I was afraid that the first protestor might have their head placed on a spike and mounted in the middle of the village, as a way to instill fear and submission in others. I certainly wouldn't put it past this savage rabble.

The villagers' faces were etched with shock. Their eyes wide, their mouths agape — stunned by this turn of events.

No one said a word. The silence in the air was eerie. I felt drained of hope. We were about to receive another hammer blow that would bring us to our knees.

Kalun released my hand — I gasped as soon as it happened.

I already knew what he was going to do.

He stepped forward and stood defiantly in front of Darrakh, who was easily a full head taller than him, and also broader in the back and shoulders. That didn't seem to deter or intimidate Kalun in the slightest. He tightened his jaw with defiance.

My stomach churned with a wave of unease. A selfish part of me didn't want Kalun to put himself on the line like this, yet the practical side of me knew it might be the only option.

Someone had to stand up for the villagers and their freedom. They couldn't just allow themselves to be enslaved by these vicious interlopers.

Kalun had now taken that stand, when it appeared no one else was willing to. I was both petrified and proud, a disconcerting mix.

Darrakh arched a curious eyebrow as soon as Kalun stepped forward. He grinned, looking down on Kalun as if he were nothing more than an insect beneath his foot.

"What do we have here?" Darrakh said in an amused voice.

"I am Kalun, and I speak for this village. I intend to serve as *Preshtakar,* to defend its honor, as is written in the ancestral rites."

Kalun took a deep breath and straightened his posture. He didn't blink. He didn't falter. If he was afraid, he didn't show it.

Darrakh laughed mockingly.

"*You* are to be the *Preshtakar* — the one to defy *me?*" he roared, incredulously.

Kalun nodded, unwavering. "You heard," he stated, simply.

Darrakh shrugged casually. "Fine by me. It looks like I will not have much competition. With that ugly, scarred face of yours, it looks like someone has already succeeded in beating you to a pulp. I am happy to finish you off. With a deformed face like that, I am sure you will be relieved to be put out of your misery."

Darrakh turned briefly to address his followers. "What do you say?"

Cheers erupted among the rival orc tribe. Arms went flying up and fists pumped the air.

The previous battle chant went back up.

"*Kallak-Edah...Kallak-Edah...Kallak-Edah...Kallak-Edah...*"

I had a horrible feeling about this. But there was nothing I could do. Kalun had made up his mind, and if he stepped down now, he would only prove Darrakh's baseless claims of cowardice to be correct.

Kalun didn't waver. He would fight to the death if he had to. I knew that full well.

I didn't want to lose him. But, in the final analysis, the future of the many outweighed the fate of the one. We couldn't just step meekly aside and allow this rabble to take everything from us, especially after we had lost so much already.

Both orcs stood chest to chest, glaring daggers at each other.

Darrakh suddenly lunged at Kalun, striking him in the side of the temple with his fist.

Kalun was rocked back in surprise, but quickly adopted a fighting stance.

Both orcs let loose with their fists, pummeling each other with flying punches.

I let out a sharp gasp and winced, grimacing at every hook and punch thrown at Kalun.

I could barely watch the fight unfold, especially since Darrakh had the upper hand as far as sheer size went.

However, Kalun's smaller stature gave him certain advantages, too. He was stealthy and nimble, able to deftly avoid many of Darrakh's blows. Kalun was able to land a few fierce punches of his own — including one to the side of Darrakh's jaw that left him reeling.

Darrakh stumbled backward, his eyes rolling back in his head. Blood sprayed from his mouth and he clutched his jaw, releasing a groan of agony.

His horde of fighters suddenly quietened a little.

Kalun was panting hard from the exertion, watching Darrakh like a hawk, fully expecting his opponent to retaliate with double the vindictiveness — and that is exactly what happened.

Darrakh clenched his teeth and charged forward, barreling into Kalun and sending them both crashing to the ground.

Gasps of shock rang out among the onlookers.

Darrakh managed to straddle Kalun's torso and rain down a barrage of punches to his face. Kalun lifted his arms to block the onslaught, then violently twisted his hips, throwing Darrakh off him.

Both fighters rapidly scrambled to their feet, but Kalun was quicker. He kicked Darrakh in the chest and sent him reeling backwards, winded and clutching his sternum.

After a pause to catch his breath, Darrakh looked up at Kalun. His eyes were animalistic. He roared with wrath. The veins in his neck and temple bulged with fury.

His horde responded with renewed chants.

"Kallak-Edah...Kallak-Edah...Kallak-Edah...Kallak-Edah..."

Unphased, Kalun speedily stepped forward and threw an arcing punch towards Darrakh's face. But Darrakh ducked at the last second, which sent Kalun teetering off balance.

Darrakh seized the opportunity to crash a knee into Kalun's stomach.

Kalun crumpled to the ground, clearly in pain and heaving for breath.

Darrakh circled his prey with his arms high in the air, in a gesture of victory.

His warriors raised the volume of their chanting.

Darrakh positioned himself behind Kalun as the wounded orc attempted to rise to his feet.

When Kalun was halfway up, Darrakh sent a knee crashing into his spine, sending him falling back to his knees in agony.

Darrakh menacingly circled back around to the front of Kalun, as if toying with his prey before going in for the kill, mirroring the pendant around his neck.

"Weak, weak, weak," he shouted. "No strength, no warrior spirit. A feeble orc, like this feeble village. Both need to be put out of their misery."

He drew up his foot and swiftly kicked it directly into Kalun's face, sending him sprawling to the ground.

The villagers gasped. The invaders cheered. I screamed and clutched the sides of my head, watching helplessly in horror.

Kalun moaned and writhed on the ground. Blood covered his face and ran down onto the ground.

"Now your nose matches the rest of your face," Darrakh declared, roaring with mirth. "Nothing but a bloody, hideous mess."

Kalun raised a hand to his battered face. Blood was everywhere. All over his face, on his hands and dripping down his chest. He wiped it away from his eyes to clear his vision.

Darrakh approached Kalun to resume the attack. However, as he stepped closer, Kalun swept his foot around in an arc and kicked Darrakh's feet out from under him, sending him sprawling to the ground.

Darrakh roared with fury but was quick to get to his feet again. Kalun used the opportunity to also scramble to a standing position.

Darrakh wasted no time in resuming his attack. He barreled forward and threw a punch, his fist landing squarely in the center of Kalun's gut. Kalun gasped. His eyes widened. He clutched his stomach. The wind had been knocked out of him. He seemed to cave in on himself and nearly fell to his knees again but, miraculously, he remained upright.

I didn't know how he was soldiering on, where he was finding the strength from.

I just wanted it to be over at this point. It was excruciating to watch. I couldn't bear to see the orc I loved becoming a punching bag for a beast far bigger than he was. If that meant we lost the village, so be it, as selfish as that was. I just wanted the suffering to end for Kalun.

"First I'll take your life," declared Darrakh, arrogantly. "Then I'll take your woman. Let's see how much of a fight *she* can put up."

This comment was the boiling point for Kalun.

He raced towards Darrakh with an expression of wild fury. Kalun raised his arms, ready to strike at Darrakh, but Darrakh grabbed his arms in mid-air, cuffing his hands around Kalun's wrists before twisting them uncomfortably. Kalun grimaced, his eyes flaring with pain.

Darrakh used his considerable strength to spin Kalun around and then put him in a headlock. Kalun was trapped, unable to escape the tight grasp.

Darrakh had a belligerent gleam in his eyes. His lips were curled into a sinister grin. He had the advantage and towered menacingly over Kalun. I was afraid of what would happen next. Darrakh could snap Kalun's neck like a twig or choke the very life out of him.

This was it. The end. I desperately wanted to look away — but I couldn't. Like poor Kalun, I had to endure this until the bitter conclusion.

I felt pins and needles surging through my fingers and toes as I went numb with shock. I gasped for air. My vision blurred. I willed myself not to faint. I had to stay strong for Kalun. If he saw me fall, that would only worsen his predicament. As long as Kalun was still breathing, he had a fighting chance.

"How humiliating," declared Darrakh. "A bloody and beaten wretch just waiting to be put out of its misery. Never let it be said that we Ukangher show no mercy. I shall make this quick."

While Darrakh was preoccupied with issuing insults, Kalun acted fast. He lifted a leg and swiftly shot his foot backwards, squarely into Darrakh's knee.

Darrakh roared in pain as his knee gave way, sending him kneeling on the ground. His grip around Kalun's neck loosened and Kalun was able to wrangle himself free.

Wasting no time, Kalun spun around him and roped his hands around Darrakh's thick neck, turning the tables on him. Darrakh attempted to squirm free, but to no avail. Kalun's muscled arms held him firmly in place. I saw the steely resolve in Kalun's eyes. He would never give up his advantage.

The invading horde was now silent, eyes wide. I allowed myself to breathe again.

With one arm wrapped tightly around Darrakh's neck, Kalun used the other to grip the bottom of his opponent's chin. I realized what he was doing. It would only take a sharp twist of Darrakh's head and his neck would snap, killing him instantly. Kalun now held the orc leader's life in his hands — literally.

Darrakh twisted desperately to free himself, but he couldn't force his way out.

Kalun twisted his enemy's head slightly, indicating that any more struggle would result in his speedy demise. Darrakh huffed in frustration.

Then the strangest thing happened.

Darrakh erupted into fits of deranged laughter. Surprisingly, a moment later Kalun began to laugh along with him.

I stared at the two orcs, completely baffled, my mouth open in shock.

Kalun released his hold and reached out to grip Darrakh's shoulder, helping him up.

Darrakh, still chuckling, accepted the assistance and, with a grunt, stood up.

Kalun roped his arms around Darrakh. Both orcs gave each

other affable slaps on the back as they embraced in a warm hug.

"Well, well, well..." Darrakh boomed, giving Kalun an approving nod. "It seems this village has some fighting spirit left in it after all."

Darrakh reached out for Kalun's hand, then lifted their joined arms to the sky and turned to face the crowd.

"It is as the writings dictate," declared Darrakh. "The *Preshtakar* stands, which means there are no longer two tribes, but one."

The crowd — both villagers and the newcomers — erupted into loud cheers and howls.

I stared at Darrakh and Kalun, clapping dumbfoundedly, in utter shock. I hadn't expected this outcome at all. I was placated, but confused, at this turn of events.

I didn't know whether I wanted to laugh or cry. It was probably a mixture of both. However, the overriding emotion was immense relief after what I was sure was a violent battle to the death.

I scanned the faces all around me. Relief and jubilation abounded. The energy of the village had lightened, as if storm clouds had lifted.

"As is the custom, we do not come upon your village empty-handed," Darrakh bellowed, with a wide grin. "We have a gift."

He gestured for one of his warriors near the front to step forward. The orc he addressed was wearing a large satchel across his shoulder.

"Come forward, Grollikh," Darrakh instructed the warrior, who dutifully stepped next to his leader with a respectful nod.

The warrior opened the satchel and reached his big hands inside. He pulled something heavy out. It was round and a little bloody. An offering of meat to share, I thought at first.

The warrior didn't keep the object in his hands for long. He abruptly threw it on the ground before us, his face contorted with revulsion.

A combined gasp rippled through the village as we registered what it was that had been thrown pitilessly on to the dirt — the severed head of an ogre, its bloody mouth formed into a frown and its black eyes devoid of life, open wide with the shock of its dying moment.

I had to look away at first, quivering with unease at the memory of being a prisoner to these loathsome beasts.

Darrakh glanced down at the severed head and spat, then looked up at the crowd with a determined expression.

"This head," Darrakh began with extra gusto, "will be the first of many trophies we will win."

He turned to face Kalun, giving him a determined look. Kalun responded with a nod.

"It represents the first tiny part of our retribution against the beasts who have spilled so much orc blood. Mark my words, brothers and sisters, we *will* have our vengeance against these monsters. They will pay for what they have done with their lives — but not before suffering immeasurably."

Cheers rang out among all the assembled orcs. Everyone present took up the battle cry: *"Kallak-Edah...Kallak-Edah... Kallak-Edah...Kallak-Edah..."*

This newfound optimism and fighting spirit were desperately needed by the grieving village. At last, some hope, some renewed vigor.

Darrakh fed into the energy humming through the air, growing animated, roaring with resolve.

"Let us show that orcs do not retreat quietly into the night.

We do not cower in fear. We fight — and we conquer. Who is with me?"

The crowd absolutely erupted into wild cries, endorsing every word from Darrakh.

"Kallak-Edah...Kallak-Edah..." continued to ring out as the newcomers fully entered the village and received warm hugs from the residents.

The initiation ritual had been concluded and the two orc tribes were now united, banded together with their hearts set on victory.

Looking at these fierce new comrades and hearing the passion and resolve echoing out into the night, it felt like we were indestructible.

Chapter Thirteen

Later that night, I sat around a roaring bonfire with the other villagers and our new allies.

Kalun, his bruised face now cleaned up, was beside me. We held hands, bonding over the warmth of the fire, illuminated by the warm, orange glow. I cuddled up close to him, recalling my earlier fear that he might be taken from me in savage hand-to-hand combat. The warmth of his sturdy body put my mind at ease.

Bountiful cuts of meat were being roasted over the open flames, cooked to delicious, sizzling perfection.

Chalices of wine were shared among the community and our guests, flowing freely until our cups ran over. We were having a feast fit for royalty, welcoming the Ukanghar and bonding as one tribe. No one would go to bed hungry tonight. Our hearts and minds were as full as our stomachs — with the spirit of hope and solidarity.

The hum of excited conversation was loud, buzzing through the air.

The Ukanghar were evidently the party-loving type. They yelled with glee, danced and playfully wrestled with each other. Drinks were spilled, a few tables were knocked over, but it was all in good humor.

As Kalun and I sat next to the fire, I saw Darrakh leaving his dancing comrades to come over to us and plop himself down with a grunt. He smacked Kalun fondly on the back and gave him a lively grin.

"Are you enjoying yourselves tonight?"

"It is quite a celebration," Kalun agreed with a nod. "And exactly what this village needs. It is…invigorating. We thank you for your support."

Darrakh leaned forward. "And we thank you for your hospitality." He stared into the flames, his expression becoming more serious.

"So, we are resolved," he continued. "Tomorrow, we raid the convent and take our revenge on the ogres."

Kalun took a swig from his mug and nodded. "Aye. We must act with haste to maintain the advantage. The convent and the ogres are in league, so the convent knows full well our village was flattened by the recent attack. They won't be expecting retaliation right away."

Darrakh lifted his mug and clanked it against Kalun's. "Take them by surprise — I'll drink to that. They'll be expecting you to be sitting back, licking your wounds."

"Precisely," replied Kalun. "We can hit them when they least expect it. They also do not know we have been reinforced by your tribe. But that state of ignorance cannot last for long. Word spreads fast, and we know there is a contingent of orcs in this village who are loyal to the old order. We *have* to strike tomorrow, lest your presence becomes known and the ogres bring in reinforcements."

As the two tribal leaders discussed plans for the raid, anxiety took up residence in my heart. I wanted this plan to free the sisters to go as seamlessly — and non-violently — as possible. I couldn't handle any more spilt blood. We had to grasp every opportunity to reduce the carnage — on our side, at least.

Darrakh addressed Kalun with a spirited gleam in his eyes. I could tell he lived for excitement, for battle, for honor and for glory.

"Tomorrow — at first light, when their guard is down," he confirmed. "We *will* have our revenge and free the innocents. It will be a good day's work."

Nya sat down next to us. Apparently, she had been eaves-dropping on the conversation for the past few minutes.

"We will come with you," she interjected with resolve.

She squared her shoulders and linked her arm with mine.

"Hana and I — we know the layout of the convent," she added. "We can get you to where you need to be faster, so you aren't scrambling around and losing time trying to find your way."

I was taken aback — but also fired-up — at the proposal.

"It's true," I confirmed, without pause for thought. "The convent is like a maze. But I can weave through the building with my eyes closed. Nya, too."

Kalun sat up straight. Suddenly the merriment of the evening left his face.

"I cannot put you in harm's way, Hana," he said. "Nor you, Nya. It is far too dangerous an undertaking."

"Nonsense," replied Nya. "Without us, your odds of success are greatly diminished. Think about it, Kalun. Why would the sisters ever listen to a mob of orcs rampaging through their convent? Why would they put their trust in you?"

"She is right," I said to Kalun, gripping his arm. "Me and Nya are familiar faces, fellow sisters. They will listen to what we have to say. In the heat of battle, you need decisive action, so lives are not lost unnecessarily."

Kalun's features were contemplative. I could see the internal conflict on his face. While he didn't want to place us in danger, everything we said was the plain truth.

"Also, we now have the Ukanghar," I gently coaxed. "Our strength has been bolstered. There is less chance that we will face any mortal danger."

"Your lady's words are wise," added Darrakh. "Their knowledge could prove invaluable tomorrow. It could make all the difference. I'd be happy to assign two of my warriors to protect them at all times."

Kalun let out a long sigh. It appeared that the weight of logic was undeniable, yet he didn't have to be happy about it.

"You stay behind Darrakh's fighters at all times," he told me and Nya, sternly. "If we are compromised, you retreat — without complaint, without hesitation, without delay. Do you understand?"

We both nodded, solemnly.

"If Hana and Nya concentrate on freeing the innocents, that will leave me more time to slaughter the ogres," beamed Darrakh. "I hope to have a high tally of kills by the end of the day. Vengeance is mine."

Kalun chuckled lightly. "You will have your fill of retribution, brother. Of that there is little doubt."

I leaned back, fizzing with both renewed energy and anticipation. I suddenly felt so alive, as if my senses were heightened.

Nya cupped her hand on my forearm and gave it a tender squeeze.

"Hey," she whispered, giving me a warm smile. "I hope I didn't overstep the mark. I just thought you would be eager to help."

I returned Nya's infectious smile.

"Not at all, sister. This is what walking the righteous path actually means. It is with deeds, not words, that we define ourselves — we were always taught that. It's time to live the teaching."

"Amen, sister," Nya replied. "This is the moment we have been waiting for. The time is finally at hand."

The bonfire crackled, warming and illuminating the central square. Food and wine were in abundance. Sounds of merriment and celebration hummed through the night air.

Kalun scanned the scene around him.

"We need to be rested and well-prepared for battle," he said, glancing apprehensively at a cluster of Darrakh's warriors who were huddled together, arms draped over each other's shoulders, singing loudly. The wine in their mugs sloshed, spilling burgundy liquid over the sides and onto their chests.

Darrakh glanced at his warriors and waved his hand dismissively.

"Don't worry about them. They will be just fine. This is their way," he tried to reassure.

Kalun cleared his throat and shifted his weight. He looked slightly uncomfortable about the situation, but he didn't argue. I understood how Kalun must have felt, seeing the fighters so inebriated the night before the raid.

It highlighted the stark difference between the warrior culture of the Sherrakh-Shen — which emphasized discipline, order and preparedness — with the traditions of the Ukangher, who relied on comradery and primal instincts.

"Don't worry about it," Darrakh said, reaching over to give Kalun another endearing slap on the back. "I will tell them to cut the drinking short soon. They will be ready for the raid. You have my word."

"Of course," Kalun said, casting Darrakh a nod of approval. Then he chuckled. "If your brigade is half this energetic tomorrow, then we have nothing to worry about."

I glanced up to watch the festivities taking place around me, fascinated by the dancing and singing.

That's when I noticed Sherrine and baby Armaan, who were intently watching the Ukangher warriors letting their hair down — as fascinated as the rest of the village by the boisterous newcomers.

I was relieved to see that both mother and child were grinning, seemingly distracted from their grief, at least for a little while.

I was grateful to the Ukangher for being the source of that distraction, even if they had no idea that they were assisting in the healing process.

Sherrine's spirits were clearly lifted as I watched her begin to bounce her bubbly baby up and down in her arms, moving and swaying in time to the singing. They even started to dance along after a while.

It was wonderful to watch Sherrine emerging from her shell of sorrow.

The Ukangher, just like all other orcs, seemed absolutely enthralled with baby Armaan, with his big brown eyes, soft curls and light green skin. He was unique in this world and a source of endless fascination.

The warriors began dancing around him, focused on entertaining him and making him laugh. The baby boy squealed with delight, clapped his hands together with excitement and bounced up and down in his mother's arms, dancing along with the warriors. He even stretched his arms out a few times as if he wanted the massive warriors to carry him away with the spirit of the dance.

The warriors reached out to him, tousling his hair, lightly pinching his cheeks and making him giggle with glee.

One warrior gestured to Sherrine that he wanted to hold the baby. Sherrine nodded and offered Armaan out to him. It warmed my heart to see how gentle and compassionate the huge warrior was with the small child. He carefully danced around with Armaan protectively swaddled in his arms.

Armaan was over the moon with joy, his cheeks rosy as he beamed a wide smile back at his mother. The orc holding him and a few of his comrades even tried to teach Armaan a warrior pose — hands raised and fists balled.

To my surprise, Armaan caught on relatively quickly. He understood what the warriors were trying to teach him and raised his chubby little arms in the air, mimicking them as best as he could. He was as clever as he was cute.

Armaan's little soft hands looked completely adorable as he balled his tiny fists and did as the warriors did. He had his father's spirit, no doubt about it.

As Armaan made the gestures, everyone cheered for him and gave him the positive attention that he so desperately needed at this time. Sherrine was beaming at the sight. I could feel my heart swelling in my chest.

"Look at her," Nya whispered, leaning in closer to me. A grateful smile brushed across her lips. She pointed to Sherrine. "This is the first time I've seen her smile since...since...Narag."

I nodded, captivated by Sherrine's happiness, no matter how

fleeting it might be.

"Yes, it is incredible to see her so absorbed in the moment," I replied. "It's what she needs right now."

"Baby Armaan is drinking up all the attention, too," Nya chuckled with glee.

I smiled, too. "He's the star attraction."

I felt like Armaan would always carry the spirit of his father in his heart. It wouldn't be easy for him to go through life without Narag, but there was no question that he had a loving support system within the community.

I savored the moment, not thinking of the future or the past, just reveling in the joy of the evening and the pure, innocent elation of a baby who was adored.

A few minutes later, I noticed baby Armaan starting to rub his eyes. His zesty behavior was waning, and he began yawning. The warrior returned Armaan to Sherrine, and she walked with him to where I sat with Kalun. Nya and Vakar had joined the dancing, as had the endlessly energetic Darrakh.

"He's getting tired," Sherrine said, approaching us as she roped her arms around the baby in a loving, motherly hug.

"He was the highlight of the festivities," I said, with a doting smile aimed at Armaan.

I covered my face with my hands, playing peek-a-boo with the little tot. He showed off his adorable bottom two teeth when he smiled, giggling each time I moved my hands away from my face. He even tried to mimic me as we played, using his little hands to cover his face and exclaiming, "peekbo… peekbo…" when he removed them.

I glanced up at Sherrine. "He's so smart."

Sherrine's face brightened. "Thank you."

"You should be proud of him," I added. "We all are. More

than words can express."

Sherrine gave me a grateful smile.

"I am. He's being a little trooper," she admitted. "Everyone's kindness is so overwhelming. I can't put it into words what it means to us."

She paused to take a deep breath and wipe a single tear from her cheek.

"I promise, when I am able to…I will return that same love and kindness I have felt surrounding us," she said.

I reached out and cupped my hand over hers, giving it a gentle squeeze. I met her gaze.

"You are doing great, Sherrine. It takes time."

Sherrine looked at Armaan. "Blow them a kiss goodnight, sweetie."

The baby pressed his chubby palms to his mouth and blew us a sloppy kiss.

"Bub-bye…bub-bye…" he cackled, waving enthusiastically.

He melted my heart with his sweetness.

As Sherrine walked back to her cabin with her infant, Kalun and I were alone again.

He gave me a doting smile. His eyes were soft and warm. "Are you enjoying the evening?"

I swiveled around to face him, feeling a surge of affection. I was intoxicated by the joy in the air and feeling a little loose from the small cup of wine I had drunk.

I glanced around our general area, but no one was paying us a bit of attention. Although we were surrounded by others, for the moment we were locked in our own little private bubble.

I boldly placed a hand over his crotch region and reached the other up to stroke his cheek. He was so handsome to me, scar and all. But also noble, kind and considerate.

He gave me a curious smile, an eyebrow arched.

"What is *that* for?" he asked, his eyes trailing down to his lap where my hand hovered.

"I don't know…" I trailed off, giving him a seductive smirk. My spirits were high. "Perhaps we can have our own private party, to keep the night going."

"Right here?" Kalun's eyes widened with amusement. He continued giving me that delicious smile that made my insides feel buttery.

I chuckled. "Maybe not *right* here…"

"In the cabin?" Kalun's eyes shimmered with enthusiasm.

I shrugged, giving him a flirtatious bat of my eyelashes. "Perhaps…"

"You are a wild woman," Kalun said, practically salivating over me.

"I am?" I pretended to be innocent.

I wanted him — in every way possible. Tomorrow we were both putting our lives in danger. But we had tonight, and it was full of possibilities.

My pulse began to race as we gazed deep into each other's eyes. I felt rejuvenated in mind and body. I craved Kalun. Naughty, erotic thoughts pounded in my mind.

"Are you up for it?" Kalun asked.

"What makes you think that?" I said, playfully.

"Well, for starters, you have your hand on my cock," he replied.

I chuckled. "It's not *technically* on your cock. It's just resting on your lap."

"I want it to be on my cock," Kalun said, breathlessly.

I stared into his eyes, unwavering. He didn't look away, either.

"I can touch your cock if you want me to…and taste it," I whispered, trying to be as seductive as possible.

Kalun swallowed hard, his eyes clouded with lust and longing. "I would love that very much. Almost as much as I love you."

Was it even possible to resist?

I felt his huge cock stiffening underneath his covering. I spread my fingers wide to trace its impressive girth.

His body was tempting me, taunting me…and he knew it. Kalun's eyes glimmered with primal yearning. My heart raced. I wanted him to have his way with me, no holding back, no regrets. I felt trapped in his erotic gaze — and I no plans for escape.

I glanced over my shoulder. Nya and Vakar were dancing together, their arms raised up to the moon as they chanted in unison with the rest of the revelers. They looked carefree. I smiled and turned back to Kalun.

"They are so happy right now," I said, feeling dreamy myself.

Kalun chuckled, giving them a fond glance. "They will be out here partying well into the night, but Vakar will be ready for battle tomorrow. My warriors know where to draw the line."

Talk of the imminent battle focused my attention back on the present moment — the time we all had together in the here and now. I wanted to enjoy this night with Kalun as if it were our last one together. I didn't want to think about the possibility that it might be exactly that.

I subtly rubbed the immense bulge protruding from under his covering. It excited me to feel the hardness of his shaft, tracing its shape with my fingers. He was solid as stone, even under the battle armor. Kalun's cheeks were flushed with arousal.

He gave me a tantalizing smile then leaned in and kissed my neck. His breath was warm on my flesh. His lips brushed up against my skin as he showered me with affectionate kisses. He traced his way up my neck to just underneath my jaw. His lips felt like velvet caressing my skin.

"That feels so good," I admitted, feeling breathless already, riled up emotionally, becoming adventurous.

"Good," Kalun said, whispering in my ear, stripping me of every mental burden I carried.

The bonfire roared, stretching up to the canopy of twinkling stars. Orcs joined hands around the flames, singing traditional songs of joy. Hope and togetherness flooded the air — and entered my heart.

I gazed deep into Kalun's olive eyes. He pushed a loose strand of hair behind my ear and buried his face into my neck again.

My breath quickened. My pulse drummed through my ears. I felt hot and flustered all over. It was amazing how a warrior so tough and domineering on the outside could be so tender with me when the time was right.

"The raid is tomorrow," I said, feeling more alive than ever. "We should get you fired-up — in the traditional way."

Kalun stared at me adoringly, softly grazing my cheek with his thumb. He was focused on me as if I was the only person in the world. He paid no attention to the revelry taking place around us. He only had eyes only for me, and I loved it. He made me feel like there were only the two of us, everything else around us melting away, including any thoughts of tomorrow.

I traced his muscular chest with my index finger. My cheeks burned hot. I leaned in and kissed his lips, sighing contentedly.

Kalun stood up. I gave him a vivacious smile as he gazed down at me. The flames of the bonfire reflected in his irises — alongside his burning desire. He looked at me as if he wanted to take me right there and then, as if the primal beast within him was being unleashed and he was powerless to control his urges. The thought thrilled me.

He quickly reached for my hand and I enthusiastically took his. He drew me to a standing position and pulled me close to his body. I felt the rhythm of his strong heartbeat thundering in his chest.

He glanced over his shoulder. Nya, Vakar and the others were still happily dancing the night away.

"Let them have their fun," Kalun said.

I squeezed his hand and gave him an enticing smile.

We left for the cabin hand in hand. I was nervous, but excited — reminding myself that sometimes you had to throw caution to the wind and seize the moment.

By the time we reached Kalun's cabin and entered inside, my pulse was drumming noisily through my eardrums.

Kalun closed the door and led me to the living room. He sat me down beside the hearth and lit the logs in the fireplace. The room was soon aglow with a warm, ginger light that made me feel cozy and relaxed.

He gently sat down next to me on the floor and began caressing my shoulders, rubbing out the knots and tension.

"You are more beautiful than words can describe," he whispered, softly.

He stared at me as if he were hypnotized. My breath caught after each gentle stroke, every tender brush of his fingertips against my flesh.

I fed into the intimacy of the moment. "You are everything I have ever wanted," I confided.

Kalun leaned in and kissed me, while gently stroking my inner thighs.

I felt my spirit soaring. I was *so* enamored with him. I wanted to know all of him. I wanted to feel his hard cock wedged between my legs, buried deep inside me, to become one with him. I wanted to gasp and rake my fingernails across his back, screaming his name as he made me come. I wanted to snatch the opportunity before it had a chance to escape.

Kalun traced his fingers up my body and cupped my breasts in his large hands. He kissed me again, his tongue gently probing my mouth.

He lifted my tunic over my head. I was now naked, warmed by both the fire and the burning desire inside me.

"Do you like what you see?" I whispered.

Kalun nodded, eyes wide. His gaze scrolled hungrily across every inch of my body. He looked like a hunter who had locked in on his target — and I was happy to be his prey.

"You are simply Heavenly," he said, eagerly.

He placed his hands on my shoulders and gently laid me down on the floor beside the fireplace. He kissed my inviting mouth while his hands roamed where they wanted to, exploring the landscape of my body.

He started at my neck and moved down to my sensitive bare chest, before trailing slowly southward. He canvassed my pert breasts with his mouth as his hands moved down. I arched my back and gasped as he sucked on my nipples and flicked his tongue across their surface. They hardened like stone under the exquisite onslaught of his soft tongue. I let out a high-pitch moan of sheer delight.

Kalun sat up and gave me a concerned glance.

"Am I hurting you?" he asked, brow furrowed.

I shook my head, panting hard. Adrenaline was coursing through my veins.

"No. I love it. Keep going. Don't stop." My voice was a husky, pleading whisper.

With a relieved smile, Kalun leaned down and trailed a row of soft kisses from my breasts down to my stomach.

My body tingled, feeling electrified with anticipation of what was to come.

His mouth skirted across my skin. His hands roamed freely. He rubbed, stroked and caressed the full length of my body, leaving not a single part untouched by his hands or gentle mouth.

When his lips reached the bottom of my stomach, he stopped.

I didn't know why he had paused. Maybe it was to drive me crazy. If that was his intention, it was working. I could feel my pussy becoming wet and warm. He knew exactly how to make me burn with lust from the inside out.

"Why did you stop?" I asked, panting for breath.

I craned my head up, just enough to see his face. He was grinning from ear to ear.

"I just want to see your beautiful body one more time before I taste you," he said.

I rested my head back down and moaned involuntarily with longing — my inner thighs were trembling and my clit was pulsing with blood and lust.

Kalun was moving at his own pace, taking it slow to heighten the anticipation.

I was desperate to feel the softness of his lips on my pussy. I could practically *feel* his huge tongue slowly licking my clit. I was losing control — and he hadn't done anything yet.

"Kalun...please..." I trailed off, begging him to go down on me before I died of unsatiated desire. I was barely able to contain myself. *"Please*...I want you *so* much..." My voice was an urgent invocation bursting from my lips.

Kalun gently brushed my inner thighs with his fingers before leaning down and trailing a line of kisses from my knees all the way up to my soaking pussy.

I spread my thighs wide, giving him an open invitation — it was an offer he gladly accepted.

The tip of his tongue began gently exploring my warm folds of flesh before he used it to spread my pussy lips apart. I moaned and arched my back, digging my heels into the floor as his tongue slowly entered my inviting hole.

Kalun slid his powerful tongue into me, wiggling it around to explore all the corners and crevices. It felt like Heaven to have his warm, long tongue lodged deep inside me, probing my most intimate areas. I was panting hard with euphoria.

I cupped my hands around his head and trailed my fingertips across his scalp, coiling my legs around his torso. I tried not to shake, but ecstasy consumed me and I began quivering involuntarily. I was swept away by the pleasure as Kalun darted his thick, muscled tongue in and out of my throbbing pussy at speed.

At the same time, he reached his hands up and cupped my breasts, softly squeezing them before using his fingers to gently rub my nipples in a circular motion. They hardened even more under his delicate touch.

I noticed his sweet, earthy scent filling the room. I breathed in deep and my lust and longing was ratcheted up. Kalun's delicious mating scent was intoxicating my senses. The aroma was enough to drive me wild but, combined with the way he was hungrily devouring my wet pussy and working my sensitive nipples with his fingers, it simply took my breath away.

My clit pulsed, engorged with blood and craving his expert touch.

As if he could read my mind, Kalun slipped his tongue out of my warm pussy and began gently probing my sensitive nub, rubbing it in circles with the tip of his tongue. I moaned with raw, primal pleasure.

Kalun fed into my cries and made me delirious with bliss as his enormous tongue continued to slide across my clit. He began flicking it urgently, sending spasms of pleasure radiating out from my center. Then he began kissing my damp pussy, all the while teasing my rock-hard nipples.

Kalun put me in a trance with his tantalizing kisses on my crotch. It felt fantastic. His lips were smooth and delicate, hitting all the right spots and sending a powerful quake of pleasure tremoring through me. The sweetest energy rippled throughout my body as he inserted his tongue back into my welcoming pussy.

Kalun slipped his hands under my lower back and used his considerable strength to lift me into the air, with his face still planted between my legs. He then slowly rocked his body back and lay down on the floor, with me straddling his face. Not once did his tongue stop lapping my hungry pussy — his sheer brute strength was remarkable.

He paused briefly to give me a naughty smirk as I looked down on him, his intense green eyes glimmering with excitement.

"I hope you don't mind being repositioned…but I was craving doing this to you," he said in a dreamy voice.

"Not at all, my love," I replied, breathlessly.

He wasted no time in re-inserting his powerful tongue deep into my wet pussy. I raised my head to the ceiling and moaned as I felt it penetrating me *so* deeply. This position allowed him deeper access to my pussy and the sensation was electrifying and mind-blowingly intimate.

I pushed my hips down onto his face as he darted his tongue the farthest he could reach inside me. He hit a pleasure spot on my back wall that sent spasms of ecstasy radiating out. His delicious scent was becoming more potent, fueling my wild abandon.

I was breathless, wiggling around on top of him as he held me in place with his big hands. He reached around and firmly squeezed my backside, before giving it a firm smack, sending a heady mix of pleasure and pain rushing through my body. It was a thrilling sensation.

I urgently rocked back and forth on his mouth, grinding my hips into him. I felt hot and flustered, warm and creamy… utterly delicious. My heart raced with anticipation.

I was close to reaching climax, soaring to absolute sexual heaven.

Kalun stroked my backside and gave it another light smack, all the while licking deep inside my pussy and lapping up my sea of love juices — it all but destroyed me.

I bucked my hips uncontrollably on his face. A cascade of raw energy was building in my body.

He held me in place firmly as he guided his tongue into my deepest crevices, driving me crazy. His tongue had a mind of its own, exploring every wall and surface — going where it wanted without restraint.

His orc scent was powerfully potent, wafting through my

nostrils and turning me on beyond anything I could ever imagine. The scent ravaged me. I was drunk on it, ready to release the roiling energy within me.

I looked down. My wetness dribbled down Kalun's mouth and chin, glistening on his olive skin. My clit pounded, pulsing with blood. I got a head rush, intoxicated by the powerful scent seeping from Kalun's pores.

Lust burned through me, electrifying my whole body. I loved Kalun — everything about him. He was the king of my heart… and king in the bedroom, too.

I didn't know how much longer I could hold back the orgasm as his tongue and mouth expertly probed my pussy and clit.

An exquisite sensation began stirring in my belly and pulsed through my bloodstream. I was charged with building euphoria. A hurricane of lust and pleasure lashed inside me.

Kalun must have known I was close. He feverishly lapped at my clit with his tongue as if he were ravenous and no amount of licking, sucking and stroking would ever satiate his hunger.

Was it possible to die of ecstasy? Impossible — or I'd already be dead!

Kalun was savage now. He spared no mercy on my pussy and clit. They were his prey and he was going in for the kill. He worked his expert mouth until I was overcome with pleasure… until I couldn't see straight. Everything went hazy. My arms and legs began shaking. I started screaming with pure elation. The pleasure ripped through me like a bolt of energy, wave upon wave of euphoria. Yet Kalun did not relent for a second.

My extra-sensitive clit was no match for the onslaught of his mighty tongue. I thrashed my hips on top of him. He had to hold me in place as I spasmed and bucked. A thunderous orgasm was splitting me in half — yet Kalun didn't stop. He kept on vigorously and viscously slaying my electrified clit with his tongue. He kissed it, licked it, sucked it, demolished it, destroyed it. He didn't stop until I was utterly spent, panting hard, reeling from the waves of pure bliss.

I crumpled into a heap on top of Kalun's massive, sturdy body. His outstretched arms enveloped me and held me tight. He stroked my back affectionately, giving me time to drift down from the shattering climax.

He made me feel more loved, cherished and important than anyone ever had. He whispered sweet endearments into my ear, showering my neck with tender kisses that sent blood rushing to my face and a tingle radiating up my spine.

"That was *so* amazing," I whispered in a breathless voice, feeling spent and drenched in sweat and my own love juices. My throat was a little sore from moaning so hard.

Kalun pulled away from me ever so slightly and grinned as we made eye contact.

"I'm thrilled you liked it but, sexy woman, I am *nowhere* near finished with you yet," he promised.

I cradled his strong chin in my hands and leaned in to kiss his warm cheek. His chin was glistening with my cum. His eyes shimmered with excitement. His orc scent was still potent, getting me worked up again.

"I want to make you feel as good as you make me feel," I said.

"You do that just by being in my life," he replied, earnestly.

I melted a little inside.

Kalun traced my chin with the tip of his index finger and gave me an endearing smile. He softly brushed my golden hair off my cheek and leaned down to kiss my collarbone. As he did, I glanced down at his swollen cock.

Kalun's heady scent wafted through my nostrils and I

suddenly had a strong urge to wrap my lips around it and taste the salty, earthy goodness. His sweet mating odor had inflamed my senses and I found his huge cock *so* enticing. It was rock-hard, meaty, veiny and incredibly alluring. It was almost beckoning me to touch it, lick it, suck it, swallow it.

My pussy tingled, sending me a request. It needed that beautiful, massive cock inside it, but I wanted to get him harder and even more aroused first.

I eyed him seductively and snaked my fingers softly around his shaft. Kalun inhaled sharply then let out a long breath. I gently stroked his cock up and down, feeling it pulse and vibrate in my fingers. It engorged in my hand, standing prouder and feeling firmer.

I slowly leaned down and wrapped my soft lips around the tip of his shaft. Kalun groaned as I ever-so-slowly moved by mouth up and down. I wanted to take it slow — to give him maximum enjoyment. I wanted him to savor the moment, to make it seem like it was going to last forever.

I let all my inhibitions go. I wasn't the same person I had been when I first joined the convent, or when I left it. I wasn't the same woman who had escaped the ogre caves. I was a woman in love — part of a special union of body, mind and soul.

My lips slid delicately up and down Kalun's imposing shaft. He was so enormous that I had trouble getting all of him into my mouth, but I took in as much as I could, relishing his huge shaft filling my mouth as I took him deep into me.

Kalun grunted with elation as I slowly brought my mouth back up to the tip of his delicious cock. His silky pre-cum was glistening and translucent, wetting my lips and dribbling down my throat. I probed the slit at the top of his cock with my small tongue and lapped up the sweet, salty and earthy fluid, then wrapped my lips back around his pulsing shaft.

I made a tight seal and then slowly lowered my mouth, swallowing him down. Kalun reached out and gently cupped the back of my head in his large hands, cradling me as I went down on him with eager enthusiasm.

His inner thighs shook. He was laying down flat now, his erect cock rock hard and pointing proudly up to the ceiling. I knelt down at his side and used my soft mouth to thrust up and down on him, hoping I was making him feel amazing.

I was living life in the moment, uninhibited, and loving every adventurous second of it.

The strength of Kalun's mating scent increased, as did the amount of precum escaping from his tip. It felt warm, delicious and soothing as it slid silkily down the back of my throat.

Kalun gently encouraged me by using his hands to nudge my head deeper between his legs. I loved the feeling of giving up control to him, so he could guide the speed and depth of my thrusts as I swallowed him down.

I wanted to impress him and make him feel as good as I possibly could. I loved him so deeply.

I took him down my throat as far as I could without feeling uncomfortable, then sucked him all the way to the top again, before slowly edging my way back down his proud shaft.

Kalun's groans became louder and more urgent.

He guided my head faster now, but not forcefully, as I bobbed my mouth up and down on his huge cock. It was my pleasure to bring him unrelenting pleasure.

I craned my head upwards to eye him seductively as I licked his swollen shaft from top to bottom, relishing the way it made him quiver with uncontrolled joy.

His olive cheeks were flushed. His breathing was ragged. He looked like he was going to reach the point of no return. I wanted him inside me before that happened.

I sat up and smiled, watching his wide chest rising and falling as he panted hard.

"I want you Kalun…" I said, trailing off, holding my breath. I didn't think I needed to explain it any further.

Kalun propped himself up on his elbows and gave me a curious smile. "Really? Are you sure?"

I nodded. "Surer than I have been of anything…I want to feel you inside me." My cheeks burned. Adrenaline rushed.

Kalun sat up and cradled my chin in his hands. He leaned in to kiss me. His scent filtered into my nostrils, enhancing the love and desire I felt for him.

"Kalun…I love you. I want you…and I want this," I reassured.

My hand reached for his giant cock. It throbbed with excitement, bulging in my hand with anticipation.

"I love you too, Hana," he replied. "You are incredible, and I want to make you feel incredible."

I smiled. "Believe me, you do that every day. Every time you look at me, I know I'm safe, adored and protected."

I stroked his cock urgently. He kissed me with frantic passion, vigorously massaging my tongue with his, while tenderly stroking my back. He was so nurturing, even in the height of passion.

Still kissing me deeply, he picked me up in his burly arms and carried me into the bedroom, where he lay me gently on the bed. Our lips were locked and our tongues danced together the entire time.

I gazed dreamily into his eyes. "Only you, Kalun," I whispered.

I took a deep breath, feeling warm and tingly all over. Love and lust had come together to form a powerful torrent of emotions. I was ready to do this — no turning back. I wanted to give my flesh, my heart, my soul.

Kalun hovered over my body, a flame of desire dancing in his eyes. His smile was mischievous. He placed my arms over my head and cuffed his fingers around my wrists, pinning me to the bed.

His cock pulsed wildly as it pressed up against my leg, flooding me with arousal.

"I am going to make you forget your name, Hana," he said with a gleam in his eye.

I craned my head up and kissed his full lips.

"Who's Hana?" I replied playfully.

Kalun gave me a look of adoration.

"I will take it slow. I will not hurt you — I promise," he reassured.

I nodded, inhaling deeply, then slowly releasing the breath.

Kalun positioned his hips lower and guided his long cock between my legs, driving me wild with anticipation.

He leaned down and brushed his mouth against mine, our lips touching delicately.

"Only you," he said as he very slowly brushed the tip of his cock against my pussy lips, grazing them tenderly before gently pushing them apart.

He probed the opening of my pussy with his swollen tip before ever-so-gently entering me.

I gasped and melted into his arms, carried off to another place both mentally and physically. I was relishing every new sensation.

Kalun took his time. He was gentle and considerate, studying my face for any signs of distress.

The lake of wetness between my legs ensured that he slipped in without resistance, even though his width filled me completely. It felt so intimate and special.

Seeing the bliss etched across my face, Kalun buried his cock deeper inside me, little by little. I arched my back and moaned, drinking in the heady mating scent flooding from his pores.

He was so huge, it took my breath away.

Kalun groaned with pleasure as he pushed himself deeper and deeper inside me. Two bodies had truly become one.

"This feels like Heaven," he whispered breathlessly into my ear, pressing his chest close to mine as we began to grind our hips together, finding a slow rhythm.

Kalun kissed me passionately and then lightly grazed his fingertips up and down the side of my body. All the while his cock was rhythmically thrusting in and out of my welcoming wet pussy, making me feel incredible.

He began to thrust a little harder and faster.

"Just let me know if I need to slow down," he said.

I cradled his head in my hands. "It's wonderful the way it is," I assured.

It had taken me a minute to find my rhythm, but Kalun's hard cock felt so good wedged deep between my legs as he pumped me with vigor.

Always adding affection to the mix, Kalun hugged me tight to his body, pressing us so close together that I felt our hearts thumping in unison.

I spread my thighs wider before lifting my legs and placing the heels of my feet on his lower back, allowing him unrestricted access to my wide-open pussy.

Kalun responded by thrusting harder and deeper, spearing

me over and over with his mammoth cock. Pleasure rippled through my body in waves as his swollen tip hit pleasure spot after pleasure spot on my back walls while he ploughed me relentlessly.

"Oh God, yes," I whimpered, encouraging him on.

He began ramming me even harder — his cock was practically a blur as he thundered in and out of me using his tremendous strength. The feeling was indescribable.

Kalun raised the stakes by taking my nipple into his mouth and sucking it eagerly before flicking his tongue over the hard surface, sending ripples of ecstasy through my chest. They combined with the currents of pleasure radiating out of my pussy and my body was enraptured with euphoria. I lifted my head and let out a short scream to release some of the roiling energy that was threatening to explode out of me.

As Kalun's heady scent filled my nostrils, I spread my legs even wider. I didn't want him to hold back. I wanted him to fuck me until I couldn't see straight — to ravage me like a wild animal that had no control.

I raked my nails down his wide back. The sensation spurred him on, as his thrusts took on a new primal ferocity. He was unleashing the beast within himself, and I was loving every second of it. He speared me so deep and hard that I had to gasp for breath, my eyes wide with the intense energy coursing through me. I screamed again — a long, guttural howl of abandon.

I was skirting the edge of climax, but Kalun lived up to his previous statement — he was nowhere near finished with me yet.

He reached under my body and cupped my buttocks in his large hands before picking me up and hoisting me into the air, all the while still wedged deep inside me. I wrapped my arms around his neck for support and pressed my chest close to his, his cock buried all the way in my welcoming, tight pussy.

Grinning, he stepped off the bed and moved me over to the wall. He held me in place with his hands cushioned under my bare bottom and, after a lingering kiss between us, began thrusting into me with vigor. The combination of gravity acting on my body and his fierce upward thrusts allowed him to spear me deeper than ever.

I gasped and stiffened, leaning in to inhale his orc scent as his cock found its rhythm inside my soaking pussy.

He gently rocked me against the wall. My head and bottom bumped up against it, but it didn't hurt, and part of me embraced Kalun's primal roughness.

"Are you okay?" Kalun asked, eyeing me inquisitively, but he didn't stop his long, deep thrusts into me.

"I'm more than okay," I whispered, breathlessly. "Keep doing exactly what you're doing."

Kalun took my encouragement to heart. He squeezed my butt cheeks tight and grinded me with fevered, passionate strokes.

His cock was swollen and throbbing, filling every inch of me, making me feel amazing. He showered my neck with frantic kisses before gazing deep into my eyes. His irises flickered with lust and longing as he pounded his rock-hard shaft inside me at frenetic speed, sparing me no mercy. The wild side of his nature had control now and I savored every incredible moment of it.

Kalun buried his face into my neck again, devouring me with kisses, while spearing me again and again with his huge cock. I squeezed my arms tightly around his neck and pressed my chest up against his, opening my mouth so our tongues could feverishly dance together.

Waves of heat and uncontrolled euphoria began building in my pussy, rippling out throughout my body. I was on the edge of climaxing. I lifted my head and released a guttural moan.

My body longed for sweet release, but Kalun wasn't done with me, not by a long shot.

Still speared deep inside me, he carried me to the living room. We bumped into furniture and knocked things off shelves in the course of our frenzied lovemaking.

I roped my arms around his neck and held him tight, both of us laughing as we unceremoniously trashed the room with our tornado of sex.

Kalun pressed me into the wall again, while holding me up. He was ridiculously strong.

The window was open, bringing in a soft breeze and the sounds of celebration and merriment outside, as well as the heady smell of the bonfire mixed with cooking food. The world seemed jubilant and harmonious. For the first time in so long, my heart was filled with joy.

I leaned in and kissed Kalun deeply. Our hips grinded together. Kalun's thrusts became harder, faster, deeper, stronger. I inhaled his powerful mating scent and looked into his intense, olive eyes. I saw affection mixed with steely resolve. This was it. There was no going back.

We continued staring deep into each other's eyes as his thrusts became even harder, faster and deeper. He was ramming into me at breakneck speed now, while searching my soul with his eyes. The level of intimacy was breathtaking.

The roiling energy within me couldn't be contained. The world blurred around me. My mouth opened and a cry of ecstasy burst from my lips. I stiffened, gasped and then waves upon waves of euphoria ripped through my body as I was consumed by a thundering orgasm.

I came with such fevered intensity that I couldn't see straight. I couldn't breathe. Every muscle in my body seized. I gasped for air, ravaged to the core, literally splitting in two from the intensity of the pleasure. The climax hit me so forcefully, it was like I was possessed.

Kalun held me firmly in place, his features etched with determination to bring me unrelenting joy. His intense gaze deep into my eyes never wavered as he continued spearing me over and over with his beautiful cock, all the while studying my face, fascinated by how the climax was ravaging my very soul.

I raked my nails up and down Kalun's back and squeezed my thighs around him like a boa constrictor. That was all it took to send him over the edge. He groaned, stiffened and then shot a torrent of warm cum deep inside my pussy. The sensation was breathtakingly intimate as his life essence gushed inside me, filling every crevice, before slowly escaping out of me, feeling warm as it ran down my thighs.

Kalun started grinding me with slower, more tender thrusts. I loved the fact that he kept going, his still-erect cock gently sliding in and out of me, exploring the lake of wetness between my legs, helping me to gently come down from the ferocious climax.

Panting hard, I buried my head into his shoulder and began weeping. I could not explain why exactly. It wasn't due to sadness, but a mix of emotions ranging from overwhelming love to relief to contentment. I closed my eyes, wrapped in his swaddling embrace. He stroked my hair and we rocked back and forth like that gently — with him still buried deep inside me — for what seemed like an eternity.

"Shall I prepare a bath?" Kalun murmured in my ear, finally. "The water might help soothe you."

I leaned back and stared into his eyes, appreciating the way his gaze reflected such profound love and empathy.

I tightened my arms around his neck and pressed my naked breasts to his chest. "I would love that."

A short while later I stepped into the bath. The water lapped around my lower legs. It was warmer than I had been expecting, but part of the sensation might have been due to my own body heat from the activity we had been engaged in earlier.

Kalun stepped into the bath with me, towering over me. His cock looked massive even dangling loosely between his legs. He tenderly swept the hair off my neck and gave me a look of adoration before leaning in to kiss me gently on the lips and wrapping me in a hug. I swooned, enveloped in his compassion embrace.

He took my hands and we slowly lowered ourselves into the water. Orc tubs are simply enormous and we had no trouble fitting inside together. The water sloshed around us, enveloping our legs and rising all the way up to our waists. It felt so soothing and relaxing to be submerged in the hot water. I let out a long, satisfied breath, practically feeling the tension melting out of my muscles.

We lay there for a while, at opposite ends of the tub, enjoying the relaxing, warm sensation and looking adoringly at each other. As Kalun's eyes scanned my naked body, I noticed a growing hunger reflecting in his irises. Was he ready for round two? Feeling rejuvenated by the water, I could feel a flame slowly rekindling in myself, too.

As Kalun's eyes continued to scroll my body, his cock grew erect as blood and lust rushed in. His engorged shaft suddenly popped up out of the water, standing proud. Feeling bold and playful — and yes, I admit it, proud that I could elicit such a response in him — I stretched my legs out and wrapped the soles of my feet around its thick head. A wide grin spread on Kalun's face as I gently massaged his shaft up and down with my feet. It was becoming harder and longer under my touch, growing to its massive fully-erect grandeur.

I took my feet away and stared wide-eyed at his thick, veiny and oh-so huge cock. It looked magnificent, the water cascading off its surface. That small flame within me suddenly grew into a blaze.

Impulsively, I pushed myself off the bathtub and moved towards him. I coiled my fingers around his glorious shaft and then guided his tip towards the entrance of my thrumming pussy. I moved closer to him, his cock gently sliding inside me as I did so. Kalun in turn moved towards me, impaling me all the way. I gasped and wrapped my legs around his torso.

Kalun groaned, his eyelids fluttered, a look of bliss was etched on his face.

"You feel amazing," he murmured, breathless and quivering a little with excitement. "This is home to me."

That statement affected me deeply. It felt so loving, un-guarded and intimate.

Kalun roped his hands around my lower back and began gently rocking his hips.

Arousal swelled within me as his swollen shaft lightly grazed against my clit. I moaned as he began thrusting a little faster, rocking me back and forth in time with his rhythm. It felt so special to be in this setting, with half of our bodies submerged in the warm water, the waves lapping up against our flesh.

I opened my legs wider, allowing Kalun deeper access inside me. His cock was as hard as steel, making me feel delicious inside. He cupped his hands around my bottom and pulled me closer in, so I was now straddling him, still submerged in the water.

He began thrusting into me harder, more urgently. I bounced up and down on him, riding him as if he were a raging bull. The water sloshed around us and over the sides of the bath. My body felt electrified as his cock speared me at speed. I leaned in towards his body and ran my tongue across his nipples, flicking, teasing, sucking hard. He let out a moan of sheer delight, his heady mating scent releasing from his pores.

Kalun ran a finger from my neck all the way down my back, past my tailbone, before gently resting on the tight little pucker of my ass. I gasped. This was a new sensation for me — and a new level of intimacy. Kalun looked into my eyes for feedback. I gave him a curious smile.

Reassured by my response, he ever-so-gently pushed his finger into me, while still thrusting his cock deep and rhythmically into my pussy. All the while he was studying my face for any signs of distress or apprehension. He needn't have worried.

It felt amazing. So warm, sensitive and intimate. The water helped to ensure there wasn't any discomfort. Kalun's orc scent heighted my lust and I instinctively pushed my hips back, so his finger speared my virgin ass even deeper. Taking a cue from my move, Kalun gently slid his finger in and out of my ass, going deeper and faster with each thrust, all the while studying my face for feedback.

I gave him a wicked grin before leaning forward and feeding my tongue into his warm mouth. Encouraged, Kalun rammed my pussy and ass with increased enthusiasm. It was a thrilling sensation to have both my holes pounded simultaneously as our tongues danced together feverishly.

I couldn't hold it much longer. It was all too much. Too intimate. Too wild. Too pleasurable. The potency of his mating scent floored me. I was barreling — body and soul — towards a ferocious climax.

I broke our lip lock and looked deep into Kalun's eyes. I noticed a frisky, mischievous gleam in his iridescent green irises.

"You do not get off so easily," he said, playfully. "There is one more thing I have dreamed of doing with you."

I would do anything for Kalun, go anywhere with him. I was his, entirely.

"I'm yours," I gasped. It was all the explanation that was needed.

Kalun grinned, his eyes gleaming with excitement and anticipation. He gently slipped out of me, picked me up and turned me around, propping me up against the edge of the basin so that my breasts were pressed against the interior. I gripped the rim of the tub and propped myself up.

He knelt behind me and gently spread my legs before wedging the swollen head of his cock between my engorged pussy lips. He gently pushed his way in, but only the tip, leaving me gasping with anticipation.

He stroked my back lightly with his fingertips, grazing my spine. Pulses of pleasure coursed through my body at his tender touch, making me shudder with arousal.

"You have no idea how gorgeous you are, Hana," Kalun said softly, his scent now more potent than ever.

His hands explored the landscape of my body, lightly skirting my legs, back, shoulders and neck before trailing to my underside to caress my breasts.

He trailed his fingertips back down my body until they reached my bottom. He tenderly cupped my ass cheeks in his hands and gave them a gentle squeeze. I could feel tingles all over my body where his hands had just been.

"You are so perfect to me," he said, lovingly, as he slowly pushed his rock-hard cock inside me inch by glorious inch. This position allowed him to reach deep inside my hungry pussy, filling me completely, stealing my breath as I gasped.

He began to grind on me again, using gentle thrusts at first to ease me into this position.

He held my hips with his hands, guiding his cock slowly to begin with, then faster and deeper, increasing the intensity.

Kalun rubbed my back as he fucked me. His cock went deeper than it had ever reached before, hitting pleasure spots I didn't even know I had. I cried out with euphoria as he mercilessly pounded me, burying his swollen cock as deep as it would go, slamming his muscular thighs against my bottom.

I loved every amazing second of it. It felt naughty and wild for him to be fucking me from behind, like an untamed animal. It somehow thrilled me that I couldn't see his face or any part of him, but could feel his powerful cock ramming into me over and over again. I closed my eyes and focused on the power and precision Kalun was using to fuck me so hard and fast, sending spasms of pleasure radiating out from my sensitive pussy. A sensual heat was building deep within me.

Kalun raised the stakes by reaching down and using a hand

to cup my breasts, squeezing them tenderly before using his fingers to gently play with my nipples, flicking and teasing them, turning them as hard as stone under his masterful touch.

He leaned down and trailed a line of gentle kisses up my neck. I turned my head towards him and our tongues danced together in the air. All the while he was mercilessly pounding my pussy with this thick, long cock.

He reached his other hand between my legs and found my swollen clit, stroking and caressing the engorged nub as his hard cock rammed me.

I was teetering on the edge. The waves of pleasure radiating out simultaneously from my mouth, pussy, nipples and clit formed a tidal wave of pure ecstasy that threatened to rip me in two. My whole body was shaking from the sexual energy roiling within me.

Yet Kalun didn't relent — he did the exact opposite in fact.

He fucked me harder and faster like I was a ragdoll, his hips practically a blur as he pounded ferociously into my pussy. At the same time his fingers pressed down hard on my clit and worked it in furious circles. His other hand squeezed my nipples firmly, rubbing and teasing them, while his long tongue snaked further into my mouth, exploring every corner and crevice. He was attacking me from all angles — in the most delicious and sensual way — and I was completely and utterly destroyed.

I defied any women alive to endure that sexual onslaught from this giant beast of an orc and not hurtle uncontrollably towards the hardest, fiercest, sweetest climax they had ever experienced in their life. It was simply impossible — and I was no exception.

I came spontaneously and uncontrollably, gasping for air,

slaughtered with pleasure from the inside out. My pussy, clit, nipples and mouth felt on fire as waves of euphoria enraptured my body and soul. It was an earth-shattering experience.

As I was engulfed by the thunderous climax, Kalun did not relent or spare me any mercy. Harder he fucked me, faster he teased my electrified clit, more vigorously he flicked my sensitive nipples and deeper he probed my inviting mouth with his powerful tongue.

I lost awareness of who and where I was, the world melted away — I only knew all-consuming euphoria and animalistic lust as this beast ravaged me ruthlessly and relentlessly. Word cannot come close to describing the torrent of bliss that elevated my body and soul.

Kalun suddenly released his mouth from our intense lip-lock.

"Hana…I am going to come," he whispered breathlessly in my ear, still pounding me deep and hard.

"Oh Kalun…" I whined, biting on my bottom lip.

I swiveled my head around to face him. He had an intense fire in his eyes. He looked frantic. He thrust so hard that my naked breasts bounced wildly. The water sloshed around us, flopping out of the basin and onto the wooden planks of the floor.

"Do it, *please,*" I said, arching my back in anticipation. "Fill me up. I want to take every drop of you."

His eyes were wild with excitement. He looked elated to hear me make that simple plea.

I snaked an arm around his neck, pulled him in and kissed him lovingly, then gazed deeply into his eyes.

He pounded me harder, his huge cock drilling me with renewed ferocity. He groaned and then his body stiffened.

In the next instant, I felt a flood of a warm cum exploding inside me. The fluid shot out from his cock and gushed deep inside my welcoming pussy. I moaned with satisfaction, relishing how warm and abundant it was.

I held his gaze as he unloaded into me. It was an incredibly intimate and vulnerable moment. I saw a mix of passion, love, lust, concentration and joy in his eyes. I was flooded by the strength of our connection in that special moment.

He had released so much cum that I felt it oozing out of me, running down my thighs in warm rivulets and mixing with the water. Kalun looked flushed and dazed, his eyes shimmering with joy, relief and tenderness. I was overcome with the love I felt for him.

He tried to gently slip his cock out of me.

"Don't," I said, looking deep into his eyes, pleadingly. I pushed my hips back so he was once again buried fully inside me.

He raised a curious eyebrow — but I was resolved and adamant, my instincts were taking over.

I wanted his cock to stay buried completely inside me. I wanted his sperm to remain deep inside my pussy, to gush and rush into every corner and crevice — to work its elemental magic inside my body. I wanted this *so* fiercely that I found myself crying gently, overcome with such powerful feelings in the moment. It was difficult to explain.

I sniffed then lifted my head defiantly and pushed my hips back even further. I was insistent. This giant orc's mammoth cock and warm, creamy cum were staying inside me. I would not let them out. They had work to do.

Sensing my desire and realizing my intention behind it, a look of astonishment crossed Kalun's face. He took a moment to process his thoughts and then smiled elatedly, before pressing himself forward, pushing his still-erect cock deep into my body.

His hands caressed my back and hips as he remained wedged deep in me. I could feel his long cock gently pulsing and spasming inside me as Kalun made an effort to shoot his last spurts of cum deep, deep inside my pussy. I wouldn't let any of it go to waste.

Kalun leaned down and kissed me passionately, scrolling his hands across my body. We stayed like this, kissing and caressing, for what seemed like a blissful eternity.

Finally, Kalun gently slipped himself out of me and rested his back on the basin. I turned around and did the same. As we collapsed into the now lukewarm water, it was like a tsunami in the bath. Half the water spilled out onto the floor, but neither of us cared. We would worry about cleaning up later. For now, we were exhausted and satiated, savoring the bliss of the intense connection of body and soul. I wrapped my arms around his torso and placed my head against his beating heart.

"Wow," I said after a couple of minutes. "I could never imagine in my wildest dreams I could feel *that* incredible."

Kalun stroked my arm.

"Incredible is the correct word," he replied, dreamily.

The water had become tepid now.

Kalun slowly stood up then reached for my hand, bringing me to a standing position too. My legs felt weak and wobbly. Once the bathwater was drained, Kalun brought fresh water that had been heating so we could wash ourselves off. He helped me step out of the bath and brought me a large cloth. He then dried me off, gently caressing every inch of my body, stroking my skin with such affection and care.

"You are so soft," he said, his voice low, his eyes cloudy with exhaustion.

"Come, my love," I replied, taking his hands and guiding him to the bedroom.

We barely had the energy to throw open the covers and climb inside the bed.

Kalun snaked his muscular arms around my body and pulled me close, our clean skin pressed together. He felt warm, sturdy and protective. His cock, now at half-mast, pressed up against my thigh. My clit was still gently thrumming with contentment. I felt encased inside a protective bubble of love and security. My eyes felt heavy and fluttered close.

Since meeting Kalun, he had sparked new life within me. Now, after our delicious love making tonight, I hoped that he had literally done just that — sparked new life within me.

With the last of my energy, I crossed my fingers under the covers before sleep swiftly claimed me.

Chapter Fourteen

Dawn rays illuminated the landscape, revealing a scene that took my breath away.

Rows of upon rows of orc warriors stood in line next to each other, their shoulders squared and their expressions resolute.

The village guards with their distinctive leather battle dress and horned helmets stood shoulder to shoulder with the Ukangher fighters, who wielded their fearsome war hammers and towered into the air. It was a sight to behold.

My heart pounded with pride to witness the two tribes banded together in solidarity.

Just last night they had been freely celebrating but now, as the first light of day bathed the land, they looked like a focused fighting force intent on victory.

Spirits were high. The assembled warriors bolstered each other with slaps on the back, bear hugs and the clanking of weapons together.

I stood with Kalun at the front of the army. He was handing out last-minute orders to the vanguard troops, who would attack first when the time came.

"Don't they look intimidating?" Nya said, approaching me from behind with an invigorating grin. Her chestnut hair was tied in a ponytail and her eyes sparkled with exhilaration.

I returned her energetic smile. "Indeed, sister. They are quite the force."

We were both wearing specially-made battle attire to match that of the village guard.

Upon realizing that Nya and I were coming along on the raid, Vakar had hastily instructed the village armorer to work through the night to prepare protective clothing for us. Each piece had been created with precise attention to detail, even at such short notice.

We wore thick leather jerkins with sharp tusks protruding from the material as well as protective shoulder and wrists guards.

Nya held up her arms at her sides and took a step backwards.

"Do I look ready to take down Vitora and the Senior Sisters? Perhaps even an ogre — or two?" she teased, her eyes bright and mischievous. Her cheeks were flushed a brilliant rose color.

I cast her a warm smile. "Without a doubt. I wouldn't want to cross paths with you."

I put my hands up in a boxing stance and took some playful jabs in the air.

"Do I have the warrior spirit?" I asked.

Nya's eyes twinkled, endearingly.

"You look like vengeance incarnate," she replied.

We both chuckled, then Nya's face slowly turned more somber. She placed a hand on my shoulder.

"However today unfolds, just know it has been my honor

to call you sister, Hana," she said. "Not just in the eyes of the Almighty, but from the very depths of my heart. I will never forget what you did for me in the convent."

I placed my hand on her shoulder, mirroring her gesture.

"And it continues to be my privilege to call you sister, Nya," I replied. "Your strength is like a shining beacon for all the sisters, especially me."

Today would undoubtedly turn into a grueling battle, and we had to be prepared for any outcome. However, looking out at our imposing army and the determined expression etched on every face, I couldn't help feeling a swell of optimism that we would be triumphant.

Villagers had gathered behind the warriors to see us off and wish us a swift victory. The atmosphere was upbeat. Optimism and confidence buzzed in the air.

I glanced at Kalun, who now stood before the assembled fighters. His chin was held high; his features were focused, engraved with iron determination. Vakar stood by his side.

"Today is the day we have been waiting for," Kalun announced loudly. "Today, we fight. Today, we free the innocents. Today, we honor the memory of our fallen comrade Narag. Today, we have our retribution."

A loud cheer went up among the warriors, followed by chants of *"Kallak-Edah...Kallak-Edah...Kallak-Edah...Kallak-Edah..."*

Kalun was a natural when it came to inspiring his guards. After successfully challenging Darrakh and winning back the honor of the village, you could sense he was being viewed as the de facto leader of the entire tribe.

"Today we ask each one of you to show honor, bravery and discipline," he continued. "And today we will show the world what it is to be an orc."

More loud cheers rang out among both warriors and villagers.

Kalun motioned for Darrakh to come forward. The Ukangher leader did so, flanking Kalun on the other side to Vakar. Kalun acknowledged Darrakh with a soldierly nod. Darrakh in turn cast Kalun and Vakar a deep bow of respect before stepping forward to address the crowd.

His jaw tight, his eyes were set with fierce determination. He raised his massive war hammer. My God, the weapon looked absolutely terrifying. I almost felt sorry for any ogre who had to stand in the path of its devastating swing. Almost — but not quite.

"Two tribes have become one," declared Darrakh. "We are one blood and one spirit, as it was in the ancient times. Today we march forwards with our weapons and our heads held high. We shall wipe out those who have wronged us, slaughtered our loved ones and spilled our shared blood. We are the bearers of justice and retribution — and TODAY IS OUR DAY!"

The crowd erupted into triumphant cheers and walloping claps. The riled-up warriors pumped their fists high into the air.

It was in that moment that I felt like I was on top of the world, like nothing and no one could touch us. It was a heady feeling.

I fed into the enthusiasm of the warriors and villagers around us, sending up a silent invocation of thanks that I was able to escape the ogre caves and live to see this triumphant day, to share in this spirit of kinship.

The warriors restarted their lively war chant.

"Kallak-Edah...Kallak-Edah...Kallak-Edah...Kallak-Edah..."

The rows of enormous soldiers began to rope their arms around each other's shoulders. They began swaying back and forth, heads up-turned towards the Heavens as they shouted in unison. They were fired up, inspired by the ancient chant and each other's camaraderie.

Nya faced me. Her cheeks were flushed red, her chestnut eyes aflame with excitement. An enthusiastic grin stretched across her lips. She was clearly feeling as uplifted as I was in this incredible moment of unity and passion.

She swung her arms around my waist and the two of us swayed together in rhythm with the fighters. We raised our heads and let our voices ring out loud — *"Kallak-Edah...Kallak-Edah...Kallak-Edah...Kallak-Edah..."*

The jubilation was cut short by a blood-curdling scream that crashed like breaking glass through the joyous chants.

The entire warrior troop went silent in an instant. Mouths dropped and everyone, including me and Nya, began exchanging baffled glances.

It didn't take long to find out where the tortured howl had come from.

Sherrine came charging towards the assembled orcs, to where Nya and I were standing. She was clearly distraught.

She wailed with anguish, her cheeks flushed a deep scarlet, her eyes bloodshot and red-rimmed. She waved her arms in frantic gestures, gasping for breath.

Nya and I raced up to meet her. We each took one of her arms, before the strength left her legs.

"What's wrong?" Nya asked, her eyes wide with concern.

Sherrine began pointing back towards her cabin with frenzied, jerky movements.

"Arma...Armaan....take...not in..." she trailed off in between sobs, only giving us brief fragments of information.

Nya rubbed her back and spoke to her in a soothing tone, trying to get her to unravel the explanation.

"What do you mean? What's wrong with Armaan?" Nya asked.

"He's…he's…*gone*," Sherrine finally choked out, her voice cracking. Her chin quivered. Her hands began to tremble as she cupped them over her face, shaking her head and sobbing in abject misery.

"He's…gone?" I asked. "How can that be?"

Armaan was just a baby and still learning to walk steadily. He couldn't have gotten very far.

Sherrine blinked at me through soggy tears. She took a deep breath and sniffled loudly.

"Someone *took* him," she said.

My heart plummeted like a boulder falling into a canyon.

Nya and I exchanged a look of dread. My stomach roiled with sudden nausea.

"Are you sure?" Nya asked, still trying to keep an even tone, but it was difficult. "What if he just got curious and ventured out. The sounds of the celebration or the newcomers might have piqued his interest and he—"

"He's *not* here," Sherrine cut in. "He's not anywhere."

Tears rolled down her cheeks and cascaded off her chin. My heart ached for her. I couldn't imagine the terror she must be feeling right now — especially after only just losing Narag.

"There *has* to be an explanation," I said, trying to comfort her, but my words sounded as empty as they felt coming out of my mouth.

"Did you check behind your cabin?" I asked. "Perhaps he got out the back door."

Sherrine fervently shook her head and stared at me.

"No," she squeaked. "He isn't in the back. Besides, he's never done anything like that before. He's never tried to climb out of his crib. I don't even think he can, the sides are too high for him to clamber over."

Nya and I exchanged another apprehensive look. Dread took up residence inside me.

I looked around. The feisty mood among the warriors had dissipated. The locals seemed equally crushed on hearing the news about the precious little boy. Armaan was *so* fondly loved by the entire community. I pictured his chubby cheeks, soft brown curls, toothy grin and dimpled little fists balled in the air with excitement. The image was a stab to my heart.

Kalun and Vakar, who had been listening to our conversation, approached us, their faces a mask of worry.

Kalun glanced at Vakar. "We need to search the entire village until we locate the baby."

Vakar nodded. "Agreed."

Kalun took Sherrine's hand and squeezed. His gaze was solemn.

"We *will* find him," he promised.

Sherrine wiped her tear-stained cheeks and gave him a bleak nod, doing her best to try to believe him. Her natural radiance had been crushed. Her features were gaunt, her hair was tangled. Her wilted posture made her look defeated, shoulders drooping dejectedly.

Vakar took off with several of the guards, racing across the village to find the missing boy. Nya and I did our best to console Sherrine, a woman who, through no fault of her own, was dangerously close to her breaking point.

A short while later, Vakar came racing back to us.

Nya and I were sitting in the grass, still attempting to console a distraught Sherrine, who was rocking back and forth and sobbing with her head cradled in her quivering hands.

Vakar's eyes were wide, his expression grim.

Nya gave him a bleak glance, swallowing hard.

"What's wrong?" — she asked the question as if she didn't want to know the answer.

I held my breath and gazed up at Vakar. My heart was in my throat. His pause before answering was excruciating.

"Morgut..." Vakar trailed off, out of breath and pointing over his shoulder. "He's...gone."

Nya's jaw dropped. "He's...*gone*? How can that be? He was locked securely in the prison."

She looked at me with befuddlement. Sherrine stopped crying briefly to join the conversation.

"Where is my baby?" she croaked.

Her voice was so pitiful it shattered my heart into a million pieces.

"We haven't been able to locate him yet," Vakar said softly, but it was clear from his tone that his earlier confidence had left him.

A few shouts erupted in the distance. Kalun jogged up to us. Judging by his dark expression, the news was not good.

"A few of the guards from the village cannot be accounted for," Kalun explained, with a heavy heart. His eyes trailed over each of us. "We can only surmise that they freed Morgut and then fled together...possibly infiltrating Sherrine's cabin and... .and..." Kalun didn't have the heart to even finish his sentence.

No, no, no, no...this couldn't be happening.

Sherrine wailed in utter despair.

Kalun exchanged a wary glance with Vakar.

"We were not paying close enough attention," he said. "Narag told us Morgut would have sympathizers in the village. We did not take sufficient heed of the threat."

Sherrine looked up.

"Now my baby is gone…" she croaked, breaking out in more heaving sobs. "My poor Armaan…"

Nya roped her arms around the tormented mother, cradling her tightly.

I looked around me. Every orc — warrior and villager — looked distressed and helpless. It was a sea of despair.

"I should have known better," Kalun continued, his features marked with guilt. "I heard the rumors but turned a blind eye, too busy wallowing in my own self-pity."

I stood up and squeezed his forearm.

"You cannot blame yourself, Kalun. None of us could have seen this coming," I said. "I met Morgut, remember. He is a master manipulator. And with the devastation of the ogre attack to deal with, how could you have stopped this plot?"

"But little Armaan…" said Kalun.

"He could be *dead* by now in the hands of those monsters," Sherrine cried.

I went to my knees and cupped her head in my hands.

"Don't think the worst, sister," I implored. "We cannot give up hope."

But the horrific truth of the matter was, Sherrine might be entirely correct.

We could only speculate as to little Armaan's fate.

I couldn't even imagine the nightmare Sherrine was living right now. She had just lost her beloved, and now their baby was gone — his little life only just beginning. It was all too much to bear.

Kalun turned his back to us and walked a few paces away.

At first, I was confused as to why he had done this, but then I heard the clomp of horse hooves galloping on the ground.

Kalun stood protectively in front of me, Nya and Sherrine. Vakar and Darrakh quickly stepped up beside him, forming a wall of security.

A horse and rider burst through the tree line of the forest and approached the village. The rider pulled on the reins of the chestnut-colored mare, slowing its speed.

The rider was wearing a brown robe with a large hood covering their head, obscuring the face. The shadowy figure was slender. I could have sworn that this was a woman.

The horse clomped nearer before the rider gave one final tug at the straps, bringing the animal to a halt a safe distance away from us.

The rider reached up and swiftly peeled back the hood — my heart leapt into my throat and my stomach lurched.

The cold eyes, the pale skin, the gaunt face, the flame-red hair and the callous sneer. Looking back at us was Sister Myrah, the cruel Senior Sister who had tormented me at the convent. She peered down at us with a look of disdain.

My pulse swooshed noisily through my eardrums.

"I come bearing a message from Vitora, our most holy and venerated Mother Superior," Myrah barked, pausing for effect and scanning the village with her cold eyes.

Stony silence was her only response.

"You should know that she has come into possession of a... repugnant abomination," she spat.

Gasps echoed out among the village.

Myrah grinned, showing her uneven teeth.

"Should anything happen to me while I am here on my

righteous, Godly duties, then the abhorrent mongrel will be slaughtered, neither mercifully nor quickly."

Sherrine sprang forward.

"He is *not* a mongrel, he's my *baby* — and he's innocent!" she screamed.

I had to rope my arms around her waist to restrain her. As much as I loathed Myrah, we had to hear her out. Armaan's life was in the balance.

Myrah chuckled mockingly, glaring down at Sherrine as if she was enjoying the frantic mother's pain and suffering. Knowing Myrah, this was the absolute truth of the matter.

No one said a word around me. It was eerily quiet in the village. Everyone was completely stunned and blindsided by this turn of events.

Sherrine was crying quietly, glaring with contempt at Myrah, as if she wanted to strangle the wretched woman with her bare hands. Tears streamed down her face in a river of sorrow.

Myrah pranced back and forth on her restless horse.

"*Well?*" She yelled, impatiently, arching a derisive eyebrow. "What is it to be? Are you going to try anything stupid?"

Kalun and Vakar exchanged an apprehensive glance.

After a moment, Kalun stepped forward. He glowered at Myrah with bitter resentment.

"You…have our word," he said with a disgruntled pause.

"What's that?" Myrah asked, cupping her hand over her ear.

My blood boiled. I knew she had heard him fine the first time.

Vakar cleared his throat. "You have our word — we will not harm you in exchange for the baby's safety."

Myrah gave him a self-satisfied smirk that maddened me further. She then clicked her heels to move the horse closer, but still remained a wary distance away.

"For now, your…*baby*…if that's what you call *it,* remains unharmed," Myrah declared, looking disappointed.

Sherrine stiffened beside us, grinding her teeth, brewing with rage.

"However, if you wish to keep him in one piece — as opposed to many pieces — I suggest you think twice about your little plan to visit the convent today. If you even *attempt* to set one filthy, unclean foot inside our hallowed walls, the mongrel's throat will be slit from ear to ear. No bartering, no negotiating, no exceptions."

Myrah's cold eyes let us know that she was not making empty threats.

Sherrine was trying to squirm out of our grasp to get to Myrah. The veins in her neck and temple were bulging with fury.

"No, Sherrine," Nya implored. "It's not worth it. Harming her in any way is not going to end well for Armaan."

"But my baby…my baby," Sherrine wailed. "She *can't* get away with this."

"And she *won't,*" Nya pleaded. "But don't do anything rash to put Armaan in danger. He needs you to be strong for him, now more than ever."

The Senior Sister chuckled derisively, glaring down at Sherrine, as Nya and I struggled to hold her back. Myrah leaned forward in her saddle and addressed Sherrine directly, fixing her with a taunting stare.

"Believe me, I would *love* to be the one who slays the grotesque little beast, to silence his wretched cries once and for all. He's just so grubby and…vile."

Myrah put on a display of shuddering as she described

Armaan, before continuing.

"It would be a service to humanity to send the ugly, ungodly creature to Hell, where he belongs. And rest assured, when the time comes, I'll be sure to wield the blade nice and slowly, so he has time to remember his dear mother with his final agonizing screams."

Myrah's taunting laugh echoed through the village as she turned her horse around, kicked her heels and galloped away, leaving only a cloud of dust in her wake.

We couldn't hold Sherrine upright any longer. She crumbled flat to the ground, wailing harder than ever, pounding her balled fists into the dirt. It was unbearable to witness her agony.

Kalun and Vakar approached us, stony expressions on their faces.

"Though it pains me to honor my word to those without honor, we cannot go forward with the raid," said Kalun, bluntly.

Nya and I nodded our understanding. Hot tears stung my eyes.

Just minutes ago, chants of glory and excitement were humming through the village. Now there were only sobs of despair and sorrow.

I cast a look around. Heads were hung low and eyes were stained with tears of despondency.

Even the Ukangher fighters looked stricken with utter despair.

Armaan, who had won all our hearts, who was the living embodiment of hope, tolerance and love, had been snatched from us all.

Strength left my body. I collapsed on top of Sherrine,

hugging her close, and cried and cried and cried.…

Epilogue

Lord grant me strength, courage and wisdom, for I know not what to do.

I kneel before you here in my chamber lost and lacking — a failure in every sense of the word.

I would allow my spirit to surrender completely, were it not for the incessant cries of the innocent baby echoing through the halls of this dark convent.

At this very moment I can hear the tortured infant screaming — 'Ma-maaa....ma-maaaaaa......ma-maaaaaaaa....'

Each cry is another hammer blow to my heart — a pitiful howl that will never be answered.

Yet how can someone as unworthy as me help — when I have failed in every act of righteousness I have attempted?

I became a Senior Sister to try to counter the cruelty and hatred spreading within these walls. I thought I could use my elevated position to quietly give succor to my juniors and steer the Senior Sisters back onto the righteous path. How foolish and naive I was.

My only reward has been a litany of failure...this is my confession.

I tried to stop Sister Hana from being taken by the loathsome ogre.

I collected insects from the convent's herb garden and hid them in my tunic. I grabbed a handful just before I ran my fingers through Hana's hair, as I pretended to inspect her body for the ogre. I knew that the sight of the creatures on my hand would deter the beast from taking her. It was a victory — but short-lived.

When Hana was slapped by Sister Myrah, she made the grave mistake of striking the Senior Sister back in retaliation. Myrah could not abide the humiliation. Her fury and subsequent lust for revenge knew no limits.

Even though Hana was to suffer a gruesome death in the detestable ogre 'sport', Myrah wanted the satisfaction of knowing that the caged sister had died at her hands — to take personal and deadly revenge for the indignity of being struck.

That evening, Myrah boasted to me that she had added hemlock to Hana's soup. The poison would ensure Hana suffered an excruciatingly painful death. 'She will not see the next morning', Myrah gloated.

As soon as Myrah confided her evil act to me, I told her I had urgent duties to attend to. I ran to Hana's cell, knocking the soup from her hand as soon as I entered, thus saving her life.

How I longed to tell Hana that I was on her side, that I would help her make her escape the next morning. But the risk of being overheard or being viewed through the hatch was too great. This convent is full of vipers. I could not let my guard down, not for a second.

Early the next morning I went alone to Hana's cell to escort her to freedom. It was the best time to flee as morning prayers were under way. Yet even then my plan turned to ash. Vitora, Myrah and the heinous ogre came in right behind me — at that unexpectedly early hour. My plan lay in ruins. My only sliver of satisfaction came from seeing Myrah's shocked face upon seeing Hana living and breathing.

Yet Hana was still doomed — the ogre carried her off to her grim fate.

My spirit was shattered. All my efforts had come to nothing.

So I succumbed to despondency, resigned to the darkness and despair of this ungodly convent.

Now here I kneel — my hope, my spirit and my will crushed.

But these cries, these miserable shrieks of an innocent baby cruelly snatched from its mother, have fueled me with anger and renewed resolve.

So I will try, and I fear there is every chance that I will fail again. But I cannot live with myself if I do not make an attempt to walk the righteous path once again.

So, Merciful Lord, I end my prayer with the same plea as I began.

Grant me strength, grant me courage and grant me wisdom.

Help me face danger with a stout heart and unwavering spirit.

I am lost in the storm and need your guiding light.

Should I perish, have mercy on my departed soul.

The time for action is at hand.

Your faithful servant.

Now and forever.

Sister Elisse.

***

Dearest Reader,

I hope you enjoyed reading the third book of my series.

I somehow feel compelled to offer an apology. I know a lot of readers expected a tidy and triumphant resolution for book three — but that wasn't where the story wanted to take me.

My usual opening of hoping you 'enjoyed' this book might be a little misplaced in this instance. But if you were engaged in the story and invested in the characters, if the book stirred some feelings, highs and lows, then I see that as the only true triumph as a writer.

So my apologies if I've left you a little sad. I just didn't want to tread the easy road and mechanically wheel out the safe, familiar tropes — where things are fairly predictable and the main characters are never truly in danger. I hope you can understand.

However, things are not over. Hope lives on — even if all my characters do not. Darkness and light have more to say.

Though the road may not be smooth, I am honored that you are travelling it with me.

Wishing you love and light,
Tanya x

My humble plea: as a part-time indie author with a full-time job, I would be inordinately grateful if you could kindly leave me a review on Amazon, as I have no other way of raising awareness of my work and it really motivates me to keep writing. Even just one simple sentence would be perfect.

***

This story is not over — join Sister Elisse soon for the fight of her life.

Join my little reader club for details of new releases and special offers, just go to: **http://eepurl.com/he3D-b**